THE LOST SUNSHINE A HOPE TO FIND MY?

PREETI BHATT

Copyright © 2015 Preeti Bhatt

All rights reserved.

ISBN-13: 978-1517110512
ISBN-10: 1517110513

DEDICATION

To my parent, Tara Bhatt and Dhanesh Bhatt, who have been my ultimate guidance stars. Thank you for believing in me when no one else did.

CONTENTS

1   A letter from the past   1

2   The city of dreams   31

3   The hypothetical girlfriend   72

4   The summer sunshine   83

5   My love…for you   135

6   The lost sunshine   163

7   With you…without you, still in love with you   202

8   A hope to find my? (Love again)   318

Normally writers do not talk much, because they are saving their conversations for the readers of their book- those invisible listeners with whom we wish to strike a sympathetic chord.

Mr. Ruskin Bond

ACKNOWLEDGMENTS

'The Lost Sunshine, A Hope to Find my ?' is a dream of mine that has been brought to reality with the vision and guidance of a few very special and talented people.

I am deeply grateful to Mr. Dinesh Singh. Without your support and guidance, this book wouldn't have seen the light of the day. Thank you taking up the charge when I gave up easily.

I express special thanks:

To the superb production team at power publishers who helped me throughput the editing process. I thank you all to bear with me when I was too pushy about the timeline.

To Mr. Jagdish Chandra Bhatt, control engineer at BARC. You were my first genuine reader who offered me your kind reviews. It helped me throughout my book.

To Mr. Manish Rajput, advocate. Thank you for your motivation and support.

To my parents, Tara and Dhanesh, who have not just helped me throughout this book, but throughout my life. Thanks for keeping up with my mood swings whenever I am down and out.

☐ Last, but not the least, to my loving sisters, Jyotsna and Dipti, who are not just my support systems, but my greatest critics.

CHAPTER ONE

A LETTER FROM THE PAST

A Sunday morning sun-kissed a small house that rested somewhere in the beautiful streets of the Dehradun Valley. The small valley rests in the foothills of the Shivalik range of the Himalayas, and is nothing short of paradise when it comes to greenery and scenic beauty. The valley in specific is known for its pretty girls, the Mussoorie lights that fill the hills surrounding the valley from one side, the enticing and adventurous road that journeys to the queen of hills, Mussoorie, its unmatched flora, the rainbows that fill the clear blue scintillating sky of the Dehradun Valley after each monsoon shower, and most importantly, its high end educational culture that attracts famous actors, businessmen and even politicians.

The city is the heart of Uttarakhand. It serves as a home to pilgrims and other people in search of peace and scenic beauty. It was 19th July, 2015, a usual bright sunny morning in Dehradun. The city was seeing sunlight after staying under a constant cover of the monsoon clouds for three days. The small house had a lawn with grasses that have become greener and taller. It seemed that the trees and the flowers in the lawn and garden enjoyed the fresh beams of sunlight. Sunlight fell on the pearls of fresh rain drops making them look exactly like small twinkling diamonds. The flowers sparkled in the sunlight and the birds welcomed such a pleasant day, after remaining confined to their nests for three long days. It was a beautiful Sunday morning.

The house that had lush green surroundings was based in the interiors of Dehradun, away from the hustle and bustle of the main road; and hence enjoyed silence and peace. The sky still had traces of black clouds that rested behind the edges of the mountains that surrounded the city from all four sides. The city was welcoming its first monsoon showers in the mid of July 2015.

The outside of the house was clean, calm, scenic and magical. It was like a miniature version of some posh farmhouse that stood in paradise. It also had a small garage besides a well maintained magical lawn. Plaster patches coming off the walls of the garage, reflected the negligent maintenance. Although the garage was too shabby to look at, the occupant being a cherry colored Maruti of the 2000 make, its proud driver maintained it like his very own personal Ferrari. He cleaned this unscratched cherry colored Maruti car very carefully, brushing and washing away every single patch of dirt and dust in and around the car. Soon, the car shone as brightly as the sun itself.

An opened door allowed some sunlight to enter into the inner rooms of that small house. The first small room visible in the interiors of that house, was probably the hall. An old man was reading the newspaper sitting on an armchair that looked out of place and did not go well with the other matching furniture in the hall. The hall was a typical synonym to the hall rooms that one can easily find in the houses of lower middle class families in India, especially North India. It had a small sofa set that was placed around a wooden center table. Few plastic chairs were lying in one corner of that hall, one on top of another. A small shelf in the right corner of that hall had a few paintings and also a memento of some school kids, probably in their 10th grade. A huge flower pot embellished the hall with artificial flowers in yet another corner.

The man, who was reading the newspaper in his armchair, was frequently getting irritated with the voices of two ladies. Those faint voices were coming from some other room in that same house. Once, he would concentrate on his reading and the next moment, he would jerk the newspaper away in irritation. It seemed that he disliked voices around him. After struggling to read amidst the faint voices that irritated him to a great extent, he threw away the newspaper and left the hall. He opened the door of another room closest to the hall. As he stepped inside, all that could be seen in that dull lit room was a ply bed, a small plastic chair and a round wooden table.

A deeper sneak peek into the room revealed a small book shelf placed in the left corner of that room. Numerous books were scattered in and around that book shelf. It seemed that the old man was highly literate and an active reader too. Soon, he banged the door shut to stay away from the faint voices, which were nothing but unpleasant noises to him.

Another room that stood opposite to the small kitchen was the largest room in that house. It had a double bed, a 20 inch BPL color television, a desert cooler and a ceiling fan. The room was empty and the voices were more audible here. This larger room had two doors- one opening towards the kitchen on the other side of the gallery, and the other opening to another room in which the two ladies were currently arguing about something.

    This room was the last room of that small house and the smallest of the three. However, this one seemed to be the most vibrant and lively at the moment; which otherwise would have remained silent. The room had three windows and three doors. It would seem at first that the resident was a great fan of lights and optimism. But the opposite was true, as all the three doors were tightly closed and two windows were sealed, while one facing the backyard was open, but curtained. An old woman was there with a young girl who was lying on the bed with covered face. That small room, which should have sparkled with lights and life, was the dullest of all the three rooms in that house. It just had a bed, a small table lamp and a ceiling fan and nothing else in the name of furniture or fancy decorations. None could say that it was the room of a young girl in her twenties. The old lady appeared to be in some kind of pain as the girl was being adamant regarding an issue that had crept in between the two.

"Naila, stop behaving like a child."

An old and feeble, anguished yet concerned voice of the old lady addressed the girl lying on the bed with a covered face.

"Come on and get up fast. Have your breakfast please. Don't make this horrible for you and me."

The voice insisted as it inched closer to the room's door.

"Naila, why are you so adamant? I want the food finished the second time I enter this room."The lady with an old voice departed. Silence loomed into the room and the girl remained in stillness yet again.

"Why do you come up with harshness and innovative ways to bother us again and again?"

The old lady was talking to herself as she cursed god for the various troubles that kept on peeping into her life and of her family's. She arranged another plate with breakfast and entered another room. The old man who disliked the voice of this lady and that girl was resting in that dull lit room.

"Have your food."

THE LOST SUNSHINE

Said the old lady and that old, irritated, rather dominant and aggressive man sat on the chair close to his bed and spoke,

"The same drama goes on again and again. Don't you grow tired of it?"

He looked up at the lady and continued after a silence,

"So you'll continue feeding her like she's 5 years old until death now?"

He was furious and fuming and the lady listened to every bit of what he had to say.

"She'll continue lying in that bed and do nothing to earn her living and help us with the finances?"

The lady had a zero expression as the man continued fuming while eating. He said,

"Destiny seems to be a good excuse to pretend you know!"

Before he could have continued any further, the lady interrupted and said,

"What other option do I have then?"

Her furious eyes were a clear symbol of how tired

she had grown with his sarcasm and growing hatred. He left his supper for a while as the lady continued,

"Is she supposed to be abandoned by all?"

Her questions had a hint of pain and anger.

"When the rest of the world and god has given up on her, I won't. She's my child. I would serve her until death and it makes me lose no patience. I feel like I have my little Naila back again."

Yes, the old lady was the mother of this young girl lying on the bed. She was Tara and the old man was her husband and Naila's father, whose thoughts were centered more on finances. Tara left the room and closed the door.

She spent her entire day cleaning the lawn, and washing and drying the clothes that lingered with the smell of moisture due to the humid weather for the last three days. It was a daily routine of her, struggling between the adamancy of her daughter and the irritation of her husband. In between the fierce strands of fury and aggression, Tara missed the old days when they lived happily years ago. What had gone so wrong that had changed their lives upside down?

"So my baby girl has not had food without momma?"

Tara murmured as she entered Naila's small room with two dinner plates in her hands. There she was- sitting by the side of her window close enough to the bed and spoke nothing. She had been looking out at the barren sky with sparse stars and a half hidden moon behind the clouds for hours now. She had a paper in her hands and tears in her eyes.

"Why is my life so empty?"

She spoke to her mother as she continuously gazed at the night sky.

"Why can't you let me know a piece of my past, mother?"

She was numb and cold, and it was painful to see her so anxious that night. Tara kept aside the supper and went close to Naila and hugged her.

"Listen my little one, this is nothing but a piece of paper and is not your past."

Naila jerked away her mother as she disagreed to do this all over again.

"We have been stuck with this same shit for the

last ten nights. I want to know what this piece of my past is. That's all."

Naila was hugely irritated and so was her mother. Tara rose from the bed and while losing her patience she said,

"Your father seems to be right. I have been treating you way too nicely despite of your growing misbehavior."

Tara was totally miffed with Naila. Naila said,

"I believed you, that he's my father and you are my mother. For once, believe me I remember seeing just your face in my memories and nothing else."

It was all silent with only Naila's voice in the room and that of a cool breeze.

"Believe me when I'm saying this past is bothering me and I see shadows in dreams. I don't remember this piece of my past. I see no face and hear no words. It's bothering me mother. I need to know who Taruj is."

Yes, this young girl knew no one and remembered nothing. Tara was taken aback with the rising intensity on Naila's face. She knew it would be hard now to keep it a secret from Naila for long. Tara left the room saying,

"This is just a letter and is not for you. Have your food and sleep."

She hastily left the room closing the door. Tara had many worries and questions floating in her mind even as she laid down for sleep.

"You were never like this my poor child, never."

She spoke to herself as she wept in pain and suffering.

"How do I let you know the truth when I know it will cascade you to endless pain all over again. After all, you both were soul mates."

Tara thought to herself and those bits of past soon patted the poor lady to sleep. It was morning and Tara was busy in her daily chores. Naila's anxiety and zeal did not let Tara be in peace even for a while.

"Okay, so now it's time for me to confront the truth."

Tara thought to herself. With this particular thought she raced to get the phone. She dialed a number and the person on the other side of the phone picked up and said,

"Hello."

A man's voice addressed Tara from the other side of the phone.

"Hello doctor, I'm Tara, Naila's mother. I need to meet you at your clinic this evening. The appointments are full and this is urgent."

Tara insisted and the doctor said,

"Okay Mrs. Joshi. Drop in at 5pm."

He kept the phone leaving Tara in some surety and peace.

"So, my little one is clearly upset."

Tara said smilingly as she entered the room and saw the food lying on the floor.

"How many times have I told you Naila, that not eating does not solve any problems dear?"

She questioned Naila as she cleaned up the floor. Naila gave no answer. Tara looked closely at her daughter's face. She was lying down on her left arm and had the letter placed closed to her heart. Her eyes had gone red and the pillow was wet. Tara forced her up to sit on the bed and amicably said,

THE LOST SUNSHINE

"You won and I lost."

With this much said, she enlighted up Naila's face with happiness.

"Then tell me who Taruj is and what is this letter?"

Tara looked at her poor child's face. She wiped off hints of tears from Naila's face, took the letter from her hand and read,

"Hey Miss Glass,

    These have been really bad mornings you know. Not seeing your face is so tough Naila. I miss you. Please forgive me if something has hurt you this much. Please give me one last chance. I know what has happened has hurt you, but let me change what's happened. I will meet you up at midnight, my Cinderella. I will come to take you with me and then, we shall not part again.

Taruj"

Tara's eyes caught tears as she read the letter that dated back to 10th August 2013.

"So mom, please tell me who this man is? What's special between him and me, please?"

Tara held back her emotions and said,

"The only memory you have is mine, right?"

Naila was a bit puzzled but she replied,

"Yes."

"And when you say mother, you mean mother, right?"

Tara questioned back with a lot of urge and got the answer,

"Ofcourse I do!"

"Whatever memories you gathered of mine in the last one and a half years, those are good, of us being pals in happy times. Aren't they?" Tara asked Naila with a lot of anticipation.

"Yes mother. I trust you."

Naila replied to put her old mother at ease and rest.

"Oh you know Naila, you might have forgotten your past, but some things never changed in you, darling."

Naila was ducked to the sight of her mother who seemed to be in smiles as she orated Naila's past to her for the first time.

"You were adamant. Very aggressive and stiff with whatever you wanted in life. And you and I were best friends. Since you hold my memories and trust only me, I request you to give it a last thought once again my child."

Tara left Naila anxious with this much, but she continued,

"If by night, you fail to trust me that this story will land you in pain, I promise I will let you know everything. Till night, I want you to rethink of the times you remember spending with me in the past. If those memories fail to curb your urge to know who Taruj was, I will put you off to sleep with a piece of your past, I promise Naila."

Tara somehow convinced Naila to wait until night. The poor girl said,

"Ok mother."

After being alone for the last so many years, Naila was happy that the night would unveil the mystery that had entered in her monotonous life for the first time.

The morning slowly passed by and soon it was noon. Naila spent her time imagining, what could this past memory hold? She spent her lonely hours living in the shadows of a man she had been dreaming of ever since she discovered this letter for Miss Glass in her mother's closet. Everytime she thought of the shadows of the mystery man Taruj, her soul, breath and heart were left intoxicated with a strange passion. She knew he had a part in her forgotten life, a big part. On the contrary, Tara spent the entire day thinking of the ramifications this could have on Naila. She was terrified as Naila's doctor had warned them long ago. He had said,

"If things bother her, she might collapse Mrs. Joshi. Her brain is not strong enough."

Tara knew the 'chapter Taruj' would either make Naila live again or choke her down. She was unaware of which side her past would take her to again. In between those strands of tension, the evening arrived. It was 4 pm when Tara entered Naila's room and saw the girl lost in a letter she had discovered a few days back.

"I should have never kept this letter living. It would have been better had I had the heart to throw it away."

Tara thought to herself and then said,

"Naila, I am going out for some work. Do you need to go to the washroom, my dear? I will only be back in a few hours."

Yes! The young girl Naila, she was on a wheelchair. She could not walk since her legs had lost sensations two years ago. She looked at her mother with twinkling eyes and said,

"Yes please."

Tara grabbed her daughter in her arms and placed her on the wheelchair and took her to the washroom.

"Mother, come back soon. I shall be waiting for you."

Tara smiled back at Naila. She dropped her on the bed, kissed her forehead and left.

All the way, as the driver drove Tara to the hospital, she kept thinking,

"It shall be hard to contain her anymore. A single chapter disclosed would pile up an array of new questions. Pressure on her mind could......."

She could never imagine what the ramifications could be. It was an hour long journey to the private clinic of Dr. Anil Arora- a famous neurologist of Dehradun who had been handling Naila's case of severe Amnesia for the last one and half years. He was one of the best Neuro physicians who had successfully helped in keeping Naila alive despite major complications that had crept up in her case like localized seizures, anxiety disorder and much more due to a major head trauma and deep wounds. Tara's journey ended and she reached the small private clinic where she waited for an hour for her turn. At 6 pm, she was called in.

"Hello Mrs. Joshi. I hope Naila is doing well."

Dr. Arora said as he greeted Naila's mother with a smile.

"Hello doctor, yes she has been doing well. But recently, she discovered a letter from Taruj. It has been keeping her way too anxious and eager. She is not letting the thing go and it's affecting her sleep now. I see her keeping awake for long hours and crying as I refuse to spill the beans of her secret past."

Tara looked worried as she continued,

"She's turning rebellious and is informing me that she has started getting shadowed dreams of some man and a weird city. She says she feels it's her past and is not ready to get over it."

The doctor patiently heard the whole thing and finally said,

"Ok, it means that the part of her brain that holds memories is getting hyperactive ever since she has discovered that letter from her past. It can show two effects on her."

Tara anxiously listened to the doctor as he said,

"Either she will end up digesting the shock of her past, or the brain can succumb to excessive anxiety, if not controlled and curtailed. If I tell you in medical terms, then we have kept her away from the memories of her past, since the nerves of her brain have gone weaker after that incident. She is susceptible to brain hemorrhage, incase she gets her nerves hyperactive Mrs. Joshi. However, the other side of the coin was always the fact that her gone memory could have only been revived if she would have been exposed to the people, places and incidents that had happened in her past life, and made an impact on her. We mutually chose to keep her away from those memories to keep her safe. But now, since she has discovered a piece from her past, she will not let it go. If we don't narrate the thing to her, she will get her brain stressed and over worked, trying to explore the forgotten memories on her own. This can cause huge pressure on the nerves of her brain and we might lose her. Certainly, either of the choices can now be extremely fatal."

The doctor took a moment and further said,

"We can't choose the option of keeping her in darkness anymore. It will certainly lead her to death now. We have no option now, but to take the risk of telling Naila the story of her past. We can hope that, unlike what we fear that she might not be able to handle the shock from her past, she might digest it and you might revive your daughter's gone memory once again. Moreover, like you said that she's seeing shadows of a man and some alien city, these are probably good signs. She's probably seeing Taruj and Delhi in her shadowed forgotten memories. We need to ensure now that her brain does not over work. And for that, we will have to narrate the entire story to her so that she does not stress her brain to know the truth.

But it will come your way with a lot of caution Mrs. Joshi. The moment you see her getting anxious or out of control, you will have to turn and reverse the subject to anything that will calm her down.

The best way would be asking Naila to listen to the story as a bed time tale and getting over it like a story. If anywhere you realize that she's not yet ready to take the shock of her past, do not shy down from lying to her about the truth between her and Taruj."

Hours of discussion with the doctor left Tara with a rough plan of how to satisfy Naila's wavering mind without endangering her life. She returned home at 8 pm and greeted her over excited and happy daughter. Tara had not seen Naila so excited and happy for the last one and half years.

"He was probably the only source of happiness in her life."

Tara thought to herself as Naila spoke,

"Hello mother, I tried to convince myself the whole day, but still could not trust that this piece of my past would leave me back in pain. Please let me know the truth."

Tara knew she had no option and she said,

"Naila, after dinner I would let you have a sneak peek in your past, I promise." Tara left Naila's room with a promise that she would narrate the complete truth to her daughter late at night.

Naila waited for her mother until 11 pm that night. Tara completed her household chores and headed straight to greet her daughter. There she saw Naila sitting by the window and smiling to the moon and stars. Tara realized Naila was happy and it was a good note to start with. She inched closer to her daughter and made her lay down on the bed.

"Here I bring you a lifetime tale of romance, love and passion with endless bits of twists and turns. The story is your life and the hero is a martyr who gave up his life for yours."

Tara waited for a reaction from Naila and the curious girl rose up and said,

"Gave up his life?"

She had numerous questions in her wet eyes and the excitement had turned to a horror in the beginning of the plunge itself.

Tara calmed her down and said,

"Yes sweetheart. He gave up his life like a solider passionately in love and kept you safe, untouched and unhurt. Your life is a secret wish of his that I have been nurturing on his commands in his absence."

Naila's heart sank as her mother still continued,

"He wanted you to live, to laugh and stay happy till endless times. Oh, he loved your eyes Naila. He said they had the world in them."

Tara's eyes had water and her voice was choking and cracking as she said,

"If you disrespect his feelings, his last wish, you will end up hurting his deceased soul that still aches for your happiness. Finding this letter in my closet is a hint from him that he wanted you to know about his existence. He wanted you to learn about his existence and still live happily."

Tara was scared that she might lose her daughter all the while she kept speaking to Naila.

"He loved you above his life. He loved you above all. He said he would live in your smiles and cry in your tears. He is a story you have to learn to love and still let go, my child."

Tara looked straight into Naila's eyes. They were deep, mystified and hurt with the departure of a man who was holding the key to her freshly discovered passion. Naila knew she had known this man for ages. After minutes of silence, Naila said,

"I knew this man has a part in my life. Though, I did not know that now he and I live in the same body. I feel I have one body with two souls resting in it, mother."

Naila broke down in tears and hugged her mother and said,

"I will live my life the way he wanted me to live it. I will fall in love with him through your narrations and would still learn to let him go. I promise, I will not fall away mother. Give me a chance to know that man who made me live and left the world for my existence. Bead him up in your bed time tales mother, and let him fill my empty life with happiness yet again."

Naila broke down in tears and kept hugging her mother tight. Naila's heart ached for Taruj even before she could have known her story with him. Tara kept hugging her crying daughter. After some moments of pain, Tara held herself back and said,

"I will take you to your past Naila. You will have to take it as a story and get over it and live again."

She smiled at her daughter who nodded in a yes. Tara began,

"I discovered a diary from your closet that

introduced me to your secret chemistry with your Mr. Despo two years ago. I spent most of my time reading that story of yours when you were in coma for 6 months my child."

Before Tara could have continued any further, Naila jumped on her bed in excitement and impatiently cribbed and said,

"Please give me that diary mother. I will sail through the endless waves of the romance I have forgotten in my present through that diary I had once written."

Before the girl's excitement could have dropped her in some dreamland, Tara brought her back to reality and said,

"When you came out of coma, I was worried that you might accidentally someday discover that diary and a shock from the past might kill you, which is why I destroyed it. I never had the heart to destroy the letter that you discovered though."

Naila's heart sank in deep pain and a tear rolled down her left eye. In deep sorrow she said,

"You destroyed the most precious thing that could have narrated me my past with him like it would have actually happened."

Before Naila could have gone into deeper pain, Tara said,

"I might have destroyed the diary, but the memories stay alive in my mind just like I read them a minute ago. I would let you know your love plunge the way it had happened, my child."

She hugged her daughter, who was now in some reassurance and she began,

"Those were the summers of 2009 that made you meet a man who changed your life upside down. You both, 'Taruj and Naila' were a perfect match. He complemented your attitude, you nullified his arrogance. He was a booster to your lost identity and a catalyst to your dormant dreams. You were just twenty back then."

It was a sneak peek in Naila's past that opened the door of endless dreams in her life yet again. Tara introduced Naila to a man from her forgotten life and Naila started finding his existence in her rusted memory from an abandoned lane.

For the next few hours to come, Naila kept asking her mother various questions about how he looked, how much he loved her and why did he had to leave forever? Naila's curiosity had no end.

Soon, her mother made her sleep with a promise to let her know her secret 'love-story' from the beginning till the end the very next day.

Naila slept that night with a weird feeling of falling in love with a dead man from the past yet again. That night she dreamt of him. She saw a hospital ward that day. It had the shadows of a man with a girl sitting close by. The shadows were dark and all that she could hear was,

"Hey Miss Glass, I love your eyes. You are going to kill me someday."

She woke up anxious and was breathing heavily. It was the first time she had heard his voice ringing in her ears. It was the first time that she saw the shadow of a man so close to her body. It was the first time that she could feel how his touch around her waist must have felt like. Naila knew the story had much more in the past than she thought it would have. She knew she had loved this man and his demise would not be an easy thing to live with for the rest of her long and lonely life. Naila was in love once again.

"Good morning dear!"

Tara greeted Naila and she saw the girl holding the

letter close to her heart in tears.

"Mother, I heard his voice and felt his touch in a dream last night. Why can't he just return and grab me once again?"

Naila had the pain of an incomplete romance and Tara knew the girl had started remembering bits of her love-story.

"It will not be easy Naila. He loved you beyond words. He loved you beyond ages. He loved you beyond the world could digest. It will not be easy to accept his departure as and when you will start learning and remembering your past with him. Which is why, I warned you of immense pain. But remember, this life of yours is his last wish. Your happiness and learning to let him go and move on in life were his secret wishes."

Tara's words made Naila stronger and she started finding happiness in everything around. She knew he wanted her to be happy. His wishes had started making a lot of sense to Naila by now.

"Mother, when will you begin to let me know about his entry, existence and departure from my life?"

Naila asked Tara with a lot of impatience and hope.

THE LOST SUNSHINE

"I will soon, my dear."

Tara said with a smile, but her answer did not satisfy Naila.

"When exactly will that time come, mother?"

Tara knew Naila does not have the strength to wait anymore. She said,

"I will begin to tell you your story with him from the beginning till the end tonight. But don't expect me to narrate it all in a day. I need you to give yourself time to learn about the truth and also learn the fact that the truth I shall be telling you is your past."

Naila knew what her mother means. And most importantly, why did she mean it all?

"I assure you, I shall live and surpass everything you feel might kill me. I promise."

Tara left the room with a smile. She grabbed the phone and informed the doctor about Naila's reactions to her past. She informed him that Naila dreamt and heard his voice and felt his touch. The doctor said,

"These are possibly good signs Mrs. Joshi. Go ahead with the truth now. You might just revive your daughter's lost memory."

Tara was happy after years. She completed all her work as fast as she could. It was 10 pm when Tara entered Naila's room where the girl waited for her mother impatiently.

No more ifs and buts, Tara huddled with Naila before reciting the story, and then she began,

"You were a tough child to deal with always. Your father's dominance and his aggression had made you fall in hatred with relationships when you were just twenty years old."

Naila's eyes widened with light, excitement and passion as her mother began reciting a piece from her lost, forgotten and dead memories once again.

CHAPTER TWO

THE CITY OF DREAMS

Naila was Tara's only child. She loved and adored her daughter unlike her husband, who always wanted a son. He could never value Naila's existence in their lives. Naila had fallen in hatred with relationships, marriage and love, seeing the constrained relationship of her parents. Tara had begun unlocking the secrets to Naila's past life that was six years ago.

"You were a tough child to deal with always. Your father's dominance and his aggression had made you fall in hatred with relationships when you were just twenty years old. Those were the summers of 2009 and you rejoiced the feeling of clearing the entrance examination of your dream course in your dream college in your dream city. I was very happy for you and we danced and celebrated nightlong."

Naila was listening to her mother impatiently. For all the time she talked, Naila could remember shadows from the past of those lost and forgotten memories.

"You were super ambitious, full of life, a feminist and an aspiring writer. You had loud dreams- loud enough to be conveyed to all. And most importantly, you were allergic to flirting and phobic to flirts. After convincing your father for five days, I managed to get his signatures on your admission form. After a lot of celebration, soon, the time was nearing when you had to finally bid me a goodbye to head your way to your dream land- Delhi it was."

Soon Naila drowned in the lanes of her past like they had actually happened.

"I will miss you Tara."

Naila hugged her mother while she was packing her bag carefully. It was the evening of 24th of July, 2009, and Naila had to leave for Delhi on the 28th of July, one day before her twentieth birthday.

"Don't lie now."

Tara replied as she was angry with Naila for two reasons. The first reason was that the girl was not taking Tara alongside her to drop her to her hostel for the first time. And the second- she was leaving a day before her birthday. Naila smiled at her mother's aggression, and probably, Tara was hiding a tear or two in the corner of her eyes as well. She hugged her mother and said,

"Oh Tara, you are melodramatic, but I really love you."

The lady gently unwrapped herself from Naila's arms and spoke nothing. Naila knew Tara was hurt with her decision of travelling alone to Delhi, as it also meant missing her daughter's much awaited twentieth birthday. Naila sighed and held her mother's hand, and said,

"You have already asked Mausi (Mother's sister in India, popularly called 'Aunt' abroad) to pick me up from the station. You have also fixed my private hostel in *Okhla* (A small area in south Delhi where the University Jamia is). Now why do you want to make things harder for you? Don't I know what he is going to do if you leave with me for two days?"

Naila was anxious and worried. Tara looked at her anxious face and said,

"Why do you take things this serious Naila? You have seen him behave the same since your childhood. Even then, these things affect you till now?"

Naila was silent for a while and her mother continued,

"Atleast things don't go violent now, my dear. He's not even that bad, as much as you believe he still is."

Naila disagreed and said,

"I know you had to run around him for five days so that he would sign on my admission form."

Tara looked at her daughter's furious face. She knew Naila dreaded her father's dominating memories from her childhood and had carried them in her youth as well, due to his ignorant nature. The girl further said,

"When has he been happy with things going good in my life?"

Naila had a point to which Tara had no answer. The girl further said,

"You think I am deaf and I don't hear him screaming at you day in and day out? And have I not noticed the tension that has started lingering between him and you ever since you have supported me in moving out of Dehradun? Don't I know that he is unsupportive of sending me out only because I am a girl?"

Naila was hugely disgusted since she knew her father was biased when it came to gender equality. She had turned a feminist since childhood, as she had seen a dominant man around her since her birth. It was not all. Before Tara could have even answered her questions, she further said,

"I saw him hitting you once, mother. I was five or six years old and I was hiding behind the door of your room."

Naila miffed Tara with her statement and the lady said,

"You are too young for all this Naila. How many times will you keep repeating and remembering the same things over and over again? Which relationship doesn't see ups and downs, my dear? That was the first and last time he raised his hand on me."

Before Tara could have defended her husband- Harisudan Joshi, Naila snapped and said,

"I agree, but he has always been raising his voice without fail."

Naila had seen a lot of aggression and tension between her parents and she knew that the reason was the absence of a son from their lives. She further said,

"He's a chauvinist and you are a typical Indian wife who cannot stand the truth against her husband, who is like God to wives like you."

Tara knew the discussion was wandering in the wrong lanes again. She knew her daughter's relationship with her husband could not gain flying colors as that of a normal father-daughter relationship. She also knew that Naila had tried her heart out, but her father's aloofness for Naila had always left the poor girl in search of some fatherly care. The presence of her father in her life was just curtailed to his signatures on her report card and diary when she was young, and his signatures on her admission form when she grew up. His presence was a Mirage in Naila's life and she always missed his love, which he kept in a shell or probably killed the very moment a girl was born to him.

Naila further said,

"I know if you come to Delhi with me, there will be no one around to cook for your God. So stick around and please him. Stop worrying about me."

She left her room and moved to the terrace. It was probably Naila's den that used to calm her down whenever she used to lose calm and patience. Nights had always been special for Naila since her childhood. She had enjoyed the beauty of the scintillating glittering hills of Mussoorie that used to shine brightly under the clear sky each night. Tara knew it was a bad idea to stick around Naila when she was aggressive. After all, the aggression was a genetic pass on by her father, a retired Army subedar.

Soon, the evening colors faded into the dark night that had the sky filled with twinkling stars and a smiling moon. Cool breeze fiddled with Naila's long open and black hair. She moved close to the edges of her terrace and her soul drenched in the beauty of those twinkling hills that had always fixed up her state of mind and brought her peace and happiness, since she was very small. She loved lights and anything that sparkled. Naila was always fascinated by the glittering sky and the twinkling Mussoorie lights, as they had the power to mend the worst of her temper.

Tara was Naila's closest friend alongside being her mother. She knew when the girl would calm down and when she would boil up again. She knew that the absence of her father's love despite him being alive had made a deep wound in Naila's naïve heart. She knew Naila had never shown, but his mirage existence in her life had always bothered the girl. She knew Naila's heart had always ached whenever she was reminded that her father hated her existence in their lives. She hated being judged. She hated being tagged as a burden. Those bitter experiences and cold memories had created a permanent distance between Naila and her father. The more she had drifted away from him, the more she had come closer to Tara.

Soon, the lady entered the terrace with two cups of green tea in her hands. Naila was sitting on the swing on her terrace and smiling to the fascinating glittering hills. Tara kept the tea close to the swing and sat close to Naila. The girl soon said,

"I wonder why I have never been to those beautiful hills mother. All my classmates used to tease me, you know."

Tara held Naila's hand as she knew Naila was hiding pain in everything she said. She missed travelling since childhood. Her father had shown no interest in her life and had never taken her out on any vacation. It was the first time that Naila was going to travel to Delhi. This was also one of the reasons why Tara was reluctant to send her daughter all alone for the very first time. The lady kissed her daughter's forehead and said,

"Because your father did not ever take you there, my child."

A tear dropped down Naila's eyes. It was a part of the broken childhood fancy that had just salvaged Naila's heart. Tara always wanted the pain and anger to fall away. But the girl had deeper wounds than her mother knew. She further said,

"You might not be having a loving father as that of your peers, but you have a loving mother who is your best friend too. Is that not enough, my darling?"

Naila looked at her mother who was trying to ease Naila's pain. The girl grabbed her mother's hand and said,

"That's more than enough. And I am sorry for the way I behaved in the evening."

Tara acknowledged Naila's apology and the girl further said,

"Now it is going to be the time for me to explore

the world with my vision. It's a dream that I am going to soon live, Tara. Please have faith in me. I am strong enough to travel alone. Moreover, it will keep me mentally peaceful that he'll not be after your life for days if you leave him alone. He's a frustrated man. This is why he was thrown out of his job. He's a victim of superiority complex."

Tara's heart skipped a beat as she just realized how rudely Naila had made fun of her Father's job loss. Before the lady could have yelled at the girl, she said,

"No, don't yell at me now. I know he was thrown out of the army. Unlike grandpa, who died as a subedar in the Army, my father was thrown out for misbehavior."

Tara resisted the fact and disagreed. She said,

"You were too young to judge the situation, my dear. Yes, he stays frustrated ever since he was thrown out. But he was not thrown out because he used to stay frustrated."

Naila wanted to resist her mother's statement, but the lady maintained her composure and further said,

"He was thrown out because he refused to serve a

slave to some corrupt senior officers in his wing. He refused to do unethical things in the Army."

It made no difference to Naila who just knew one thing- that her father had shown hypocrisy in bringing her up. All that she knew was the fact that he had loved her male and female cousins, but always let her down in front of others and in person. Now everything about him, his fault or not, was always his mistake for this young girl. A part in her heart had always ached for her father's love- her father who was a victim of his own orthodox personality. No doubt, he was patriotic, learned and highly efficient, but he was a failed father in the end of all. And that is all that mattered to Naila.

Tara knew it was useless to drag the discussion. So, she finally agreed to send Naila alone, but with a lot of instructions. Soon, the 28th of July arrived, and Naila reached the Dehradun Railway Station with her mother. She had her train lined at 5 pm. It was the Shatabdi Express that reaches Delhi Railway Station at 10.32 pm. Naila had butterflies in her stomach throughout the time she waited for her train. Tara had clutched Naila's left hand very tightly and soon the coolie dropped their luggage near the bench and said,

"C2 coach yahi rukega (The C2 coach will be lined

right in front of this bench)."

Tara paid him 100 rupees and soon, the mother and daughter duo, which had stayed inseparable since Naila's birth, started waiting for the train. Tara held back her tears and avoided direct contact with Naila's eyes. Naila, on the other hand, was not speaking much as she had a choking throat. On one hand, she had immense happiness of moving to the city of her big dreams. On the other hand, her happiness was burdened under the painful departure with her best friend and mother, Tara. Naila had no idea how she was going to manage in that big city and become a famous writer. She knew that the city would throw numerous challenges on her way, but she did not know how she would face them alone in the absence of her mentor mother. However, the brave girl showed nothing- not even an iota of her worries, and soon the train arrived at 4.32 pm.

The coolie re-appeared and arranged Naila's luggage near the chair number 17 in the coach C2. Tara and Naila did not say a word. It was an awkward silence. They both kept hugging each other and continued feeling each other's essence for the remaining few minutes of togetherness. When the train started to move exactly at 5 pm,

THE LOST SUNSHINE

Tara rushed down. Naila was still holding her mother's hand. And slowly, the train gained speed. Tara's hand got separated from Naila's hand that was still stretched out. Naila saw her mother getting swayed away and away. She saw tears welling down her mother's eyes. And in no time, she rushed to grab her window seat, where she sat down with sad and closed eyes. Her childhood memories and those of her youth, danced in front of her eyes and she was missing her mother dearly. Tears rolled down her eyes and soon she got a call from her mother. She picked up the phone and said nothing. The hilarious voice from the other side of the phone said,

"I knew you would cry. See, I won the bet."

Tara managed to set Naila in some smiles and the girl said,

"Promise me that you are going to stay just fine in my absence."

Tara sighed and replied,

"I promise, I'll be fine as long as you stay fine, my darling."

Naila could feel the hint of a choking throat in her mother's otherwise hilarious voice, and the lady further said,

"Call your Mausi once you reach the railway station. They'll come to pick you up at the platform itself. Don't go anywhere all by yourself. It's a huge railway station unlike the small easy station of our city. Understood?"

Naila agreed to all the instructions of her mother and soon she kept the phone. She kept looking outside the train and witnessed numerous jungles in her journey to Delhi. She had a clear aim of making big, which is why she was hitting the lands of Delhi. She wanted to be a famous script writer and an influential journalist. However, the only tough part of chasing her dreams was her mother's absence. Passing time eased her pain and she started getting goosebumps, as and when she started nearing the Delhi Railway station. She passed most of her time remembering how her father had made a negative impact on her life and also that of her mother's life. Those bitter memories remained in the swaying roads and jungles of her hometown that she had left somewhere away.

It was 10.25 pm and the train finally arrived at the New Delhi Railway Station, a few minutes early. Naila managed to drag her bag to the train's door with great difficulty. She threw it out literally as holding it and carrying it down was not easy for her. Finally, she moved down safely.

"God knows what all Tara has packed. Such a heavy suitcase this is."

The moment she took her mother's name, she got her phone ringing. As she saw the name displaying on the screen, a smile rested on her lips. She answered the call and said,

"Have you packed stones in the bag? Do you know how heavy it is?"

Tara felt easy after hearing Naila's voice, as she could sense unusual happiness in it. The lady carried the joke forward and said,

"Not just stones my dear, there are bricks too."

The girl giggled and her mother further said,

"They have arrived at the station. Have you reached?"

Naila impatiently replied and said,

"Oh, I reached just now."

Tara disconnected the call for a while to

coordinate with her sister and soon, Naila was safely received by her relatives. She greeted them with warmth, but rather felt how annoyed they were with the un-necessary trouble they had to face. Naila was not amused with their unwelcoming behavior, but she was used to the aloofness. She wondered for a while to herself and said,

"It's ok Naila. Atleast they are helping you unlike your dad."

She calmed down, and soon, she was in the streets of the city where a clear sky could hardly be seen. There were huge buildings, twinkling malls, well-lit streets, stupendous traffic control, busy roads and much more in the night lanes of Delhi. It was a city with very popular night life after all. Naila was sinking deep into the fresh feel of this city that certainly had some magic in its air. But Dehradun's ambience made Naila nostalgic at the same time. Soon, the road came to an end and Naila reached a building in *Pitampura*- the area of North Delhi where her Mausi lived with her family of two daughters, one son and her husband, in a 2 BHK flat.

The moment Naila entered the flat; she was humbled with the welcome her cousin brother offered. Her cousin sisters were asleep by the time she reached their house, at 11.45 pm. After welcoming Naila warmly, the little lad went to sleep as well. Naila was given a separate room and the complete family adjusted in one room for that night. The next day, Naila would have to shift to her hostel in Okhla anyway. She was still obliged that they had compromised to accommodate her comfortably.

As she scanned the room, it was no less big than her own room in Dehradun. She felt in place and the room had an AC as well. The hall was smaller than her's in Dehradun, but still, the flat valued two times higher than the overall property they had in Dehradun. It was the magic of being in the garb of a metro city maybe. Her Mausi asked her to freshen up while she arranged dinner for her. Naila was very keen to check the balcony and soon she made her way, and experienced how different the sky of Delhi was from the sky of her hometown.

Naila sighed heavily as she saw no stars, but just some passing airplanes. These were frequent and they filled up the unclear sky of Delhi every five minutes one after the other. She missed the clear star studded sky of her city and felt nostalgic. Suddenly, her phone buzzed and she answered the phone. It was her mother's call, who from the other side of the phone wished her a very happy birthday. It was 12 at midnight and Naila had turned twenty, standing in the balcony of a small, 2 BHK flat, in Delhi. Soon, her Mausi called her in and served her food. As she sat on the sofa to eat, she said,

"Oh, you did not have food as well?"

"We did not have time, my dear. We had to pick you up safely after all."

Replied her aunt, and she was humbled again. They had done their best to ensure that Naila was safe and comfortable. She smiled and started eating. Soon, she left to sleep and just before she would have fallen asleep, her Mausi woke her up and said,

"Hey, happy birthday."

Naila hugged her Mausi and remembered how the lady had wished her on each birthday she had spent in her hometown without failure.

"Oh, you don't forget my birthday ever, Mausi."

The lady smiled as she hugged Naila warmly.

THE LOST SUNSHINE

Naila felt the same warmth in her arms as that of her mother. The lady took out a gift box that had been kept hidden under the bed. Before Naila could have jumped and kissed her Mausi for getting her a huge gift, the lady said,

"It is from your mother. She had parceled it to me a week ago."

A tear dropped down Naila's eyes and soon the lady left her alone. Naila called up her mother and started un-wrapping the gift. It was a beautiful diary and a fancy bag, exactly the same one that she wanted from the market when they (Naila and her mother) went shopping. Naila was speechless for a moment and then she said,

"This bag is expensive."

She heard a soft sob, following which, her mother said,

"It isn't more expensive than your happiness. Happy birthday from your father's side as well."

It spoilt Naila's moment and she said,

"He doesn't wish me ever even when I am in front of him. Why do you try to fit him in the frame of my life when he likes to paint his existence black?"

Tara stayed quiet. She did not want to spoil Naila's birthday. Soon, the tired girl fell asleep and the next morning she was dropped at the Hostel where she was going to stay for the next three years of her life. It wasn't the in-campus hostel of Jamia, but a private hostel that her aunt had booked for her on her mother's persuasion. The girl was soon left alone in the five storeyed hostel that still did not have an elevator. The worst- Naila's room was on the fifth floor. The breather- her bag was dropped in her room by an in-house maid.

Naila was not sharing the room with anyone, and so, it was a relaxing welcome. She feared darkness and decided to keep the lights switched on each night, as she did not have to deal with the agony of a room-mate. Her college was going to begin from the 2nd of August. And Naila had four days to explore the shortest route to her college, the available juice and food corners in Okhla, and much more. However, she decided to stay indoors for that one day. She disliked the mess of her hostel, which was unclean, but she had no option. She stopped looking at the way the food was prepared, and like the other girls in the hostel, she carried her food straight to her room.

It was a birthday unlike her other birthdays,

when her mother used to cook special dishes for her. She sighed as she began eating the tasteless mixed veg. and dry chapattis.

"It is a part of hostel life."

Naila said trying to console herself, while crying as she missed her mother. She decided not to eat further, and rather, spend her entire birthday sleeping. The night welcomed a beautiful view from the balcony of her hostel's room. It refreshed Naila's soul as she peeped out and saw the glittering highway that was far away from the hostel, but clearly visible from the balcony of her room on the fifth floor. The twinkling blue lights in and around the *Lotus Temple* were also a welcome treat for the young girl. The Lotus Temple is situated at the *Nehru Place* in New Delhi. The breathtaking view of that beautiful temple from Naila's balcony was a refreshing moment for the nostalgic young girl. She deeply thanked her Mausi (aunt) for choosing a room that offered such a spectacular view. The yellow lights adorned the road and the sight was one of the best things Naila had seen in her small life by now.

Soon her mood was fine again, and she took a bath and decided to have dinner in the hostel's mess. She dressed up in the satin night suit that her mother had newly purchased for her. The moment she pulled the door to open it, she was shocked to realize that it was locked from outside. She screamed for help and could hear some giggles, that soon faded, and the sound of footsteps was not heard again. Naila immediately dialed the hostel's reception number, but the phone was unreachable. She tried her warden's personal number but it was switched off. She kept banging on the door for help, but gave up after two hours.

The girl did not have food since morning and was starving. She had no friends in Delhi and she did not want to unnecessarily bother her mother, who would have freaked out knowing about the ragging in the hostel. Naila tried to sleep, but could not. Her stomach was cramping and soon she got her first lesson at Delhi. She had to give up her ego and manage her hunger with the leftover food from afternoon, which she disliked. She had tears in her eyes as she somehow gulped that dry, cold and tasteless supper that night. She fell asleep soon, and in the morning, she realized that the door had been unbolted.

The moment she realized that the door was open, she registered a complaint with the warden. Following that complaint, she never faced a similar problem again. Naila felt confident now. For a small town girl who had just moved out of her house and had no friends in that metro city, it was a big incident. Following that small nerve wrecking incident, she believed that she was prepared to handle the harshness of Delhi on her own.

Naila had gone to Delhi in order to find a way out of her half-dead world. She was skinny, but she never bothered much about it. She had long black hair and she wore glasses with huge power. She didn't welcome undue attention at all, and had a big dream in her big black eyes- Naila that was, six years ago. She explored a momo (a spicy veg. filling) corner in a nearby complex in Okhla, that also had MC'd, Domino's, Pizza hut and Barista. However, the momo corner became Naila's favorite and soon she started making way for those tempting pieces of veg. fillings each evening all alone.

She kept that diary- the birthday gift from her mother, as her most treasured belonging and her best friend in Delhi. Naila would write down her entire day in the diary each night before sleeping. Soon, days started passing by and the 2nd of August came. Naila had stepped out of her house and city all alone for the first time. It was her time to explore her possibilities without her mother's extra care. She had never been very good at making friends when she was in her city, but she managed to make a thick bunch of close friends at Delhi, in her campus, from the moment she stepped in.

She certainly felt blessed to be around a bunch of thirteen more pals, who became her great friends by the end of her first inspirational lecture in her new campus- Jamia. Unlike a nervous start in the hostel, she made a confident start in her college campus. Naila had a new love in her life now- Delhi. It was also the summer of 2009 that brought her close to the pathway of raining dreams and her true love- Taruj.

Naila was now a student of Jamia Millia Islamia. Jamia's mass communication wing was Naila's department. The public central university held the key to unlocking Naila's dream of becoming a writer with a golden pen. It was one of the best Asian universities for Mass Communication and Journalism. Naila had worked very hard day and night to get into the desired course in this university to pursue her graduation. She passed her twelfth standard when she was just eighteen and it took her two years to get an admission in Jamia, for graduation in Mass

THE LOST SUNSHINE

Communication and Journalism, at Delhi- the city of her dreams.

Once Naila moved to Delhi and Jamia, she managed to make quite a few interesting friends in her new campus. Naila was certainly feeling very different and she absolutely loved every bit of her new life at Delhi. She was sailing in an ocean of endless happiness and had sky high dreams.

"Tara….. Oh Tara! I love this place. I love this life. I love this city. They are all so welcoming to my dreams."

Naila was very happy as she narrated the different colors in her life to her best friend and mother- Tara.

"That is fine, my dear, but tell me one thing- are there some good men in the campus too?"

Tara giggled as she knew that men and relationships were the two topics that bugged her daughter. Naila and Tara had a love-hate relationship when it came to the topic 'men'.

"Oh please Tara, I don't hunt men like fishes."

Naila snapped back seriously.

"That is ok Naila. But you need to get married at

some point of time or the other. You must prove to me that you are not lesbian."

Tara knew she was teasing her little daughter, but she loved it somehow.

"Look Tara, I hate this topic. And by the way, yes, I'm lesbian."

Tara shot back in a second and said,

"Oh, is it? So you'll get me a daughter-in-law?"

Naila knew Tara had serious doubts about Naila's sexuality, and so, she teased her mother back. She said,

"Yes, ofcourse I will."

She drove her mother crazy with her reply. The old lady said in a flat and concerned voice,

"So, you'll seriously marry a girl?"

"Tara, please change the topic."

Naila warned her mother as it had started irritating her. She was no more finding humor in the serious ongoing topic. Her mother said,

"Listen young girl!"

Naila understood that her mother would not let it go. Thus, before she could have come up with something new on the benefits of dating men, Naila said,

"I need to sleep early mom. I'll be going to IIT tomorrow with friends. There is some cool fest, Rendezvous, in the campus. A.R Rahman is coming over for a live show, and so, I don't want to wake up late."

Naila informed her mother and disconnected the call before the lady could have inspired Naila on the ten benefits of dating an IITian. Naila smiled to herself and slept. While the night sky conspired of intoxicating Naila's life with love, she peacefully slept unknown to what the other side of the night had for her.

After a busy day at college, Naila headed straight to IIT Delhi with her friends. She was unaware that she was about to enter the weird land of exceptionally talented brains with a nasty humor. IIT has exceptionally creative men and those men have huge eyes for women. The word impossible doesn't exist in their lives. Exceptionally shy of women, most of them underrate their looks. In a serious deficiency of the opposite gender in their campus, they go into a nutshell and find it hard to be comfortable and behave normally if women approach them. Only when they get normal around you, they show you their hidden talents in romance, flirting, humor and much more. Highly efficient of remaining loyal to a girl, they talk of nothing else other than who's the new *maal* (hot girl) in their campus.

It was a huge campus that had a maximum number of guys and a negligible number of girls, of about 0.02%. The wind, music, vodka on the rocks, shy glares from all the four sides....it was the campus of IIT-a college unlike college. IIT was like a battalion of the smartest engineering brains (mainly male brains and a few female brains) with zero confidence in front of women, but with grave lusty eyes for them. Naila had never been to such a place and could hardly handle the humor in the air. It was certainly fun, but the air had hints of undue attention all around.

Suddenly, a guy approached Naila and said,

".."

"What?" Naila replied with some surprise.

"Am I Taruj? Can I drink for you?"

He said shivering, after realizing that he was

not audible the first time. Naila gave him a stone-cold look that almost choked his heart the moment he was trying to open his mouth any further. It seemed he would soon get a heart attack. Finally, Naila excused the poor guy and left the place staring at him from head to toe.

Naila moved to a different corner, and left behind a sweating guy. Soon after Naila was gone, he was huddled with a flock of other men laughing at him and teasing him.

"The audio went missing brother. Did you secretly pee?" The bunch laughed with sarcastic comments.

"Am I Taruj? Abbey, usko kya pata tu Taruj hai ya Mohini? (How would she know whether you are Taruj or Mohini?)"

"Can I drink for you? Kya piyega uske liye bhai? (What will you drink for her, brother?)"

He was bullied endlessly until he finally managed to speak. And he said,

"One- handle a girl, two- speak in full English, what for? Free vodka for seven days! Why don't you all try the bet then?"

Taruj replied, still sweating, partly laughing and

partly panting. He further said,

"I would have kissed her, had you all not been around."

His comment only increased the intensity of the crowd's laughter. The crowd lessened and Taruj was left back with five friends of his.

"Are you crazy? Who asked you to accept the bet?" A junior of Taruj giggled and Taruj said,

"It was for free vodka."

Taruj had a lot of teeth for sure. He was daring and gutsy, but the topic 'women' made him nervous just like the fellow IITians around him.

"Bhai(brother), she raped you totally."

Giggled another friend of his and he replied,

"I escaped a slap, that's enough."

They giggled and chatted endlessly on how Taruj flunked on impressing yet another woman continuously for the hundredth time.

Naila heard most of the story and couldn't relate to the humor or the jokes, which she found to be cheap. She left the place and tried to find her friends all around, but couldn't. She tried to scan every corner of the campus, but was left with only disappointment. Naila was scared when she saw the time- it was 2 am and was certainly not the safest of hours at night. The campus was welcoming enough to her, but not enough to let her stay back the whole night.

"I'm Naila."

Naila took a man by surprise as she approached him from behind. He turned towards her but did not have any word to say- just an expression of victory (getting masked with fear).

"Don't think too much. I am not here to be kissed by you."

Naila freaked out the bunch completely. Taruj's friends ran to find some dark corners so that they could hide behind the bushes and peep secretly. He was suddenly left alone with Naila. He was silent and she continued,

"I heard you talking shit to your friends and I need to tell you that you are a……."

Naila paused for a while and thought to herself,

"I need his help, probably the only man I slightly

know in this weird place. I can't be rude to him."

She changed the topic and said,

"So, I'm new to the city and my friends have left me here. Can you please drop me back to the hostel? Safely." She added in the end.

Taruj thought to himself,

"The lottery ticket wants to know if I like money or not."

"So?" Naila questioned while looking straight in his eyes.

"Ofcourse I will." Replied Taruj and accompanied Naila to her hostel. Before they stepped out of the campus, Naila took out her phone and clicked his picture, and said,

"This is for added safety, you see. I have sent it to all my friends and family to let them know I'm with you, so that you don't end up raping me or something."

Taruj was weaving raunchy stories in his mind throughout the way to Naila's hostel. But all the while, he couldn't understand what was annoying and disgusting Naila so badly. Finally, he dropped her at the hostel and she slammed the door on his face.

While he was heading back, he received a picture on his cell with a text.

"We can show this picture to the others only if you promise to share the vodka."

It was a picture of Taruj accompanying Naila outside the IIT gate. Even before Taruj could have reached the campus, his hostel wing was filled with the stories of him being 'the dude'. The moment he arrived, he was chased by a crowd of men who wanted to know what happened.

"I told you, I would have kissed her, had you all not been around. Now, buy me and my friends' vodka for seven days." He grinned as he spoke to his fellow mates who had placed the bet with him.

"Why your friends? The bet was between you and us."

One of the seniors said, to which Taruj replied,

"But the bet was simply to impress her, not to impress her so much that she becomes my girlfriend."

He left the ladyless men anxious to know more about his fake charm that helped him lure a woman with so much ease.

"Show us proof that she's your girlfriend, we'll believe you only then."

One of the men from the crowd said and the others unanimously agreed to him. The crowd slowly started scattering. Finally, he was left back with his five friends, who chased him to hit him, saying,

"Apne sath hamaari bhi muft daru marwa di (killed our free alcohol alongside yours)."

After a good chase of fifteen minutes, they all sat down and said,

"*Fight maarte hain fir, shayad bandi maan jae* (let's try out once, maybe the girl gets impressed)."

After hours and hours of discussion, they found enough strength to send Naila a friend request from Taruj's Facebook profile. It was declined by Naila immediately with a reply,

"Do I look insane, that I'll add you?"

The hope of free alcohol was bothering the friends and the fear of being laughed at was bothering Taruj. The evening took Taruj by a surprise, when he saw Naila's friend request. He jumped on his bed and accepted the request the very next moment.

"She has sent me a friend request!"

He passed on the message to all his friends and they all huddled around his laptop in his room.

"I think she's interested in you, brother."

One of Taruj's friends was skeptic about Naila's intentions from day one when she had made him drop her back to her hostel.

Hours of discussion and motivation gave Taruj the required strength to talk to Naila online. His friends left the room and Taruj kept sitting on his laptop for hours before pinging Naila. He rehearsed how exactly he would approach Naila to impress her totally. All the while he was thinking about how to impress Naila; he got a ping from her.

"Hello."

He was thrilled to see Naila's message and in no time, he hurriedly replied,

"So miss feminist, you couldn't get over my charm?"

He said it with extreme charm and confidence in a single shot.

"Control your hormones and before you plan to get cozy in bed, let me tell you what the truth is."

Naila's flat tone, her arrogance and attitude got Taruj high everytime he faced her. While he kept on listening patiently, Naila said,

"I am sure you had a certain motive when you sent me a friend request. I heard your cheap gossip with your cheap friends that evening anyway. So, would you let me know now?"

"And I'm certain you would have never sent me a friend request without a motive either. Why don't we begin with your motive Miss Glass?"

All the while Taruj thought he was sounding very seductive and confident, he just kept on infuriating Naila. She bluntly said,

"Fine, if this makes you feel that you've won, I'll delete you from my friend list and never cross ways again."

Her reply made Taruj furious. After all, how could he let a girl delete him from her friend list so easily?

"Hey no, please wait. Yes I had a motive. I needed your help. I wanted you to be my friend so that I could………"

He sent an incomplete sentence to Naila, and she completed it saying,

"So that you could get free vodka for seven days."

Taruj smiled at her foolishness but agreed to it, and said,

"Exactly."

"Okay then, I will help you, but in return you have to fix me up as a summer intern at your campus. Deal?"

He somehow liked the arrogance, foolishness and innocence of Naila, and he replied,

"Done deal."

While Naila was furious to keep the chat word to word, Taruj was more assertive on talking matters other than business.

"So girl, how do you like our campus then?"

"Why can't you just stick to the deal?" Naila replied with rudeness.

"Don't be so rude, adamant and practical all the time. Are you using me for the summer internship?" Taruj joked.

"Excuse me? You are getting free vodka, is that not enough for you?"

Naila's reply left Taruj in a smile that refused to die. He replied,

"No, that's not enough. I need to know you as well. People should be convinced that you are my friend after all."

"Sorry, I don't have time." Naila said as she wanted to end the discussion soon.

"What's the pain?" Taruj asked in anxiety.

"You are the pain, man. Can't you just get over this and leave with the fact that a girl turned you down?" He smiled as he realized that Naila was already in a discussion with him.

"Turned me down? Get a break lady!"

His reply left Naila amazed and she replied,

"When we meet again for the internship, I'll look around for this similar confidence that you show up on chat." She dug hard to break his confidence, but couldn't win over his humor, atleast on chat.

"Listen, stop flirting, I hate flirts."

Naila was fuming but she kept on talking to him.

"By the way, Miss Glass, flirting is good for health. You need lots of it. You might just end up gaining some health."

Taruj flirted with Naila and at the same time teased her.

"Really? Now if I take this, a few days later you would come upto me and say- hey Miss Glass, sex is even better for health. Would that mean I should have sex with you? You are desperate and it shows."

As Naila replied, Taruj imagined exactly how she would have looked, had she said it face to face with a flat look.

"You win and I lose, Miss Feminist." Taruj wrapped up the argument, smiling, only to begin a new argument with her.

"Why did you hate me so much when I did drop you 'safely' (he asserted) and spoke not a single word?"

Taruj had left Naila fuming to the very thought of that night and she replied in disgust,

"You spoke nothing, your pants did."

She was clearly miffed with the very thought of that night and left Taruj in laughter. He replied,

"Ofcourse, I mean it's natural. You asked me to drop you home. What else does it mean?"

"It simply meant, drop me home. But how could you believe it. What else did you expect to happen then? A seductive room, a raunchy bikini, and dirty sex?"

Naila was clearly disgusted and Taruj enjoyed her company, and he said,

"Just the sex."

The night of chatting kept playing its beats and continued beading a story that had the essence of becoming a lifetime tale. Naila hardly realized that she gave away hours and hours just being engaged around Taruj, and said to herself,

"What a cheap guy, cheapster."

She was furious, yet she did not realize that it was Taruj who had completely taken over her mind. Taruj, on the other hand, kept on talking to himself using the slangs that are typically used by IITians. He thought,

"What a confidence she carries, man. Miss feminist keeps it flat and point to point. *Bas pain bohaut maarti hai yar* (she takes a lot of stress and takes things too personally)."

As he continued sitting in his room, he was greeted by his flock of friends who were anxious that a girl had finally chased him after ninety-nine failed attempts.

"Details to bata bhai (tell us the whole story, brother)."

Suddenly, Taruj had become the point of attraction even in his group, who now felt it was much more than 'Muft ki Daaru' (free alcohol). His fresh, passionate and intense feelings were clearly getting masked under the burden that Naila was now his alleged girlfriend throughout the campus, and even amongst his friends. He suddenly had become the leader of his dry group, and he was certainly not ready to give away the title any time soon. Once the celebrations ended, Taruj decided to go and meet Naila in person and convince her to be his girlfriend, his hypothetical girlfriend (shhhhh).

CHAPTER THREE

THE HYPOTHETICAL GIRLFRIEND (SHHH…)

Naila was already friendless again, after her friends had left her alone at the IIT campus that night. She had indulged herself in an argument with all her friends the next morning after the incident, two days ago.

"How could you all leave me alone and none of you bothered to pick up my call? Why did you all ask me in, if dropping me back was such a pain? Don't you people know I am new to the city?"

Naila yelled at her friends since she was offended about the way she had been treated by all of them. All her pals were silent as she continued speaking,

THE LOST SUNSHINE

"I tried finding each one of you throughout the campus. I scanned every little corner of the huge campus to get a glimpse of either one of you. Where the hell did you all die last night?"

Naila was clearly miffed and aggressive. One of her friends tried to calm her down and said,

"Nailu, please relax. You did manage to get back safely right? What's the point then? We are sorry dear. But we are glad you grew bold with it."

The answer did not go down Naila's spine well and she snapped,

"What the hell do you mean by that? Were we not supposed to get back together? To stay together?"

Naila was clearly taking it too far and growing impulsive and emotional (that's how she was, but it was not accepted easily by all).

"Chillax Naila. You are not a school girl and neither are we all in high school, that sitting on the same bench and being together means friendship. We are all grownups, aren't we?"

Those reactions were hurting Naila all the more. Her friends tried to calm her down and one of them said,

"Listen, we really are sorry dear. We forgot you were with us after each one of us was down with seven or eight shots of vodka. When you called us, we were totally drunk and out by then. We received your missed call notifications this morning itself."

Naila was unsatisfied with all the answers and she said,

"This is how friendships in Delhi must be then. This is not how friends are supposed to be, atleast in my city."

This was too much for the Delhites and clearly Naila took it too far. They said,

"Maybe that's why you never had many friends back in your city too."

With hints of tears, Naila left the place and two days later, she was all alone in the big campus of her college. Naila was sitting under a tree that Monday morning, when she was suddenly approached from behind.

"So Miss Glass, you like the hot weather it seems."

She was surprised as she turned around and found Taruj standing in front of her. She was more shocked to see that unusual confidence in his personality that was so unlike an IITian. He stood ahead in his trademark style- crossed legs, hands behind his head and a vibrant smile.

"How do you know where I study? Are you stalking me?"

Naila said it without a smile on her face. She showed no happy expressions of greeting Taruj.

"Well, Miss Glass, I found your details in the entry list of Rendezvous."

Taruj replied with a smile.

"What suddenly makes you so confident the hundredth time?"

Naila tried to put Taruj at discomfort, but he said,

"I have no idea, I feel easy around you."

    All the while the two continued talking, Naila felt something in her stomach. She stopped talking to him for a while and thought,

"This can't be love at all. Maybe I am emotional, friendless and alone, and that is why, I like his presence for now. Maybe that is creating a reaction in my tummy. That's all."

Taruj, in the meanwhile, kept looking at Naila. The changing expressions in her eyes, her long open hair playing around her face, he felt something for the girl for sure. Interrupting those silent sessions of falling in love, Taruj said,

"I need your help Naila."

She looked at him and replied,

"What?"

"When I woke up in the morning, I was famous in the campus and amongst my friends because everyone thinks that you are my..."

He again gave Naila an incomplete sentence which she completed,

"That I am your girlfriend, right?"

Taruj started getting nervous again with the changing expressions and tone of Naila, but he said,

"Listen, I can explain this, please."

Naila interrupted and said,

"Make sure its quick. I have a class to attend anyhow."

Taruj nodded in agreement and began,

"This is not just about free vodka anymore. If they get to know you are not my girlfriend, I will be laughed at yet again. We are already friends. Can't we pretend being in love for three months till you work as a summer intern at my college?"

He had a pleading expression on his face. Naila said,

"Why should I help you with this? The deal was of being friends."

"Then be my hypothetical girlfriend. I promise I will also come to pick you up and drop you back 'safely' for those three months. That was not a part of the agreement, right?"

Naila stopped for some while, thought something for a good ten minutes and said,

"Under a few conditions, I would help you like you want me to."

Taruj was clearly excited and he said,

"And the conditions would be?"

Naila said,

"Number one- I don't want your pants to do the talking when you stay quiet.

Number two- It would be my plan and my way to prove I am your girlfriend to the others, not yours.

Number three- You will have to help me throughout my summer internship in anything I want. You will also have to help me collect the data I would need to find, relevant to my internship. And you will have to help me get an access to the main library as well."

Naila looked at his face for a while and said,

"Say deal?" She stretched her hand forward for a hand shake and Taruj jumped to grab her hand and said,

"Done deal."

He pulled Naila closer and said,

"By the way Miss Glass, kissing is more hygienic than handshakes."

Naila pushed him away and said,

"What a Jerk."

She started walking towards the canteen and was

given a chase by Taruj. Taruj thought to himself,

"What makes me so comfortable around her? This confidence is weird. Am I not scared of being slapped?"

He enjoyed every bit of Naila's company. While the two were walking, Naila said,

"So, as an extension to the agreement, you will have to come and pick me up and drop me back daily without failure."

After half an hour of chatting at the canteen, Naila left Taruj alone and said,

"Go back now. I have my class, I need to rush."

She stood up and left for her class. After three hours, Naila came out and started walking towards her hostel alone. She stopped for a while as she saw Taruj standing by the side of a tree and waving at her. It was all very weird for Naila. She knew she was getting undue attention, but it coming from Taruj, was not pissing her off. Naila found herself smiling and then she got a hold of her emotions and started walking towards him. She said,

"Have they thrown you out of the campus for chasing girls?"

"Who?" Taruj asked her.

"IIT people, seems like you have a lot of time to bunk lectures."

Naila taunted and the two started walking towards Naila's hostel.

"So, after a week, we are getting started with the summer internship. Get me fixed as a writer and an event coordinator at your campus before that." Taruj simply kept nodding in agreement to whatever this skinny, confident and sarcastic girl said.

"Regarding your girlfriend thing, we'll have lunch together. I'll pay half my share though. You can click a few pictures and show them to your friends. That shall be enough to prove we are dating."

Taruj suddenly pulled Naila to the corner of the road in a rush. In no time, a high speed bus passed by the same spot. He immediately said,

"Atleast watch where you walk Miss Feminist. I don't want a bus to ride over my hypothetical girlfriend on the very first day of our made up dates."

Something stuck Naila's heart that very moment.

She was glued to his smile, and suddenly he said,

"Remove the condition number one please."

Naila's expression changed to one that showed deep irritation with the guy thing creeping up yet again. The two remained in touch with each other and one week passed by. Taruj kept his promise and got Naila fixed as a summer intern in his campus. A week passed by and Naila exchanged numbers with Taruj.

"Stop texting me at night Taruj."

Naila replied a night previous to the beginning of her summer internship at IIT Delhi.

"Then what else do you want me to do at night, my hypothetical girlfriend?" Taruj replied while he was giggling.

"Thank god I'm not around. Had I been, the world would have easily known how desperate you are." Naila replied in disgust.

"I bet you like it. You talk of it more often than I do." Taruj replied only to increase Naila's irritation.

"Control your hormones and let me sleep now. I have my internship from tomorrow and I don't want to be late on the very first day." Naila replied, while dodging Taruj's question.

"Don't worry, you are now officially the girlfriend of Mr. Taruj Singh. Being late wouldn't matter." Taruj replied.

"Well that suits your reputation not mine. And correction please, hypothetical official girlfriend." Naila fell asleep with her reply. The night kept passing hour after hour. Was the girl changing? Did she no more feel cheesy with flirting when it came from him? Were Taruj and his desperate story getting over Naila?

It was the very first night Naila dreamt of him. A gentle dream of her first collision with Mr. Despo made Naila happier. Fresh love was certainly in the air, with no one to catch it so early. She knew deep inside that he was the man who had started making an entry in the abandoned lanes of her heart that summer.

CHAPTER FOUR

THE SUMMER SUNSHINE

As promised, Taruj helped Naila to get a chance to work as a creative coordinator in his campus of IIT for three months as a summer intern. Naila had begun the epochal journey of love, passion, romance and zeal during the August of 2009. Initially, she found it very hard to get used to the unwanted glares and attention that the campus had for a new girl around. Taruj kept her at ease though, and now, it was Naila's turn to return the favor and prove that she was his girlfriend.

Naila took over the command and decided that she would enter the campus hand in hand with Taruj each day and would leave by evening after having snacks with Taruj in his Despo nest- his room, or the love nest like he said while teasing Naila.

The first day of Naila's internship began with the awkward feeling of holding hands with a nasty and desperate chunk. It was certainly something that was causing butterflies in the stomachs of the duo. Naila and Taruj held hands and walked through various corridors, crossing staring eyes, to finally reach the curriculum hall.

"Hey Miss Feminist, you really have soft hands."

Taruj complimented Naila, as it seemed that he had drowned completely in the feel of Naila's first touch.

"Oh really! Thanks."

Naila smiled as she said it and Taruj knew it was not all. He literally laughed at the sarcastic expression on Naila's face and held his breath as she changed her expression to a rather cold, blunt and aggressive one. She continued,

"Girls have soft hands. But how would you know that after hundred successive rejections?"

Naila had a winning look on her face as she still continued,

"The only place you have ever felt the softness of a woman's hand is on your cheek."

Taruj laughed and said,

"So, if you feel the injustice that had been done to me a hundred times, you are free to place your hand somewhere else too."

Naila's expression changed as Taruj started to get a little nastier.

"Don't let the world know how desperate you are, only if you remember condition number one."

Naila replied as she was grinding her teeth in anger. Taruj immediately left her hand and started moving away. He murmured to himself and said,

"I'm a guy, this is natural."

He looked back at Naila and said,

"See you Miss..."

He left the sentence incomplete and moved away. Naila faintly smiled and said,

"Miss Glass!"

She watched him fade away slowly as he moved towards the other side of the campus. And soon, he was gone. A busy day it was. Different stories kept floating in the air of that unusually welcoming college campus. It was like a fete of humor and brains, eager to catch some romance by luck. Naila discovered her hidden, rather recessive but existing part- love for romance writing. It was a new feeling that had kept Naila captivated. She began weaving a love plunge for the annual screenplay that she was supposed to be working on.

A spur of unusual emotions started dancing in Naila's mind and captured her heart completely. She sank in the deep thoughts of Mr. Despo who found a permanent stay in her memories now. Her pen started to bead in words an epic drama, a love saga- 'The Summer Sunshine'.

Busy spells of observing the romance in air, feeling a gush of fresh passion, catching a new story at every hidden corner of the buildings in that huge campus, were disturbed by Taruj at frequent intervals. Naila started enjoying his presence in her life even before she could admit or accept the fact secretly.

"Hey Miss Glass cum writer, may I have a look at what you're upto?"

Taruj started peeping into the papers that concealed Naila's 'The Summer Sunshine'. In no time, Naila covered her papers and replied,

"No!"

"But why? I hope my endearing personality has not spell bounded you. Let me just confirm."

Taruj teased Naila as she stayed glued to his deep black eyes for a few moments of silence. They looked into each other's eyes and no one spoke for the few moments to come.

Taruj came close to Naila and said,

"I need to confirm that you have not fallen in love with me."

He was getting spell bound by Naila's charm and her silence. It made him curious as to how she wasn't reacting to his rubbish flirting. Just to break the strands of that awkward spell she was captured by, he tilted close to her and said,

"I think you need a kiss!"

He nastily stared coming close to Naila. It broke the spell she was captivated by, and she pushed him away and said,

"You know you have some serious syndrome!"

Her disgust and anger were masking the hints of nervousness she carried from what had happened between her and Taruj just moments ago. As the evening approached, Naila agreed to have a cup of coffee with Taruj in his love nest of the hostel number 8. Room number 413 had been Taruj's home away from home, for the last three years of his life.

"So maam, welcome to my love nest!"

Smilingly, he welcomed Naila in his room with open hands. Before she could enter his room, she was astonished by a thick crowd of men who almost chased Naila and Taruj to the room. They behaved almost insanely in a fit to prove that they were behaving normally. A scary look on Naila's face, a rather aggressive one, scattered that crowd and she hurriedly took a step inside the love nest.

She was stunned to see a rather messy, small room that had posters of playboy trying to gulp some air beneath the huge piles of books and magazines.

"Why did you remove the playboy posters from the walls?"

Naila's questions had no full stop and she continued,

"It is clearly evident that the posters trying to peep

out and catch air are freshly removed."

She passed on the sarcastic comments as she took a 360-degree turn and scanned the walls of the room.

Taruj laughed as he realized how witty Naila was. He said,

"What else did you expect then? A double bed with roses, well lit candles, champagne, light music and chocolates?"

"Just the bed, with no roses."

Naila replied and Taruj offered her a seat on the bed next to him.

"Come, have a seat." He said, while pointing out at the empty space on the bed.

"Where? Over the dirty clothes or the playboy posters?" Naila snapped at him while she was still scanning the room.

"Don't worry, there are no cameras." Taruj said while he gently smiled at Naila.

"Oh don't you worry. I have ways to find out hidden cameras as well." Naila replied as she still continued scanning the room.

"Do you have lasers in your eyes?" Taruj joked just to make sure that Naila could start feeling comfortable. She took out her phone, dialed a random number from her contact list and placed the phone in and around every possible hole she could find in that room. After inspecting the room for the next thirty minutes, she finally sighed and grabbed a small chair that was lying close to the door.

"Are you fine, Naila?"

Taruj questioned as he figured out hints of tension on her face. She was speaking less and watching more.

"Yes." Naila replied as she was still scanning the room for something.

"What do you plan to do as such that you need an assurance that there are no cameras around?"

Taruj joked just in order to get the cat out of the box. But in vain, Naila was hugely uncomfortable. She was desperately waiting for the next thirty minutes to pass by before she could get out of that room. Soon, the next half hour passed. She stood up and rushed to grab the door. The moment she pulled it to open, she was startled by men falling almost over her. Taruj dragged her back unhurt, and eventually, the crowd disappeared.

On the way back, she was silent. Taruj dropped her at the hostel gate and she never looked back even once.

Naila kept thinking of Taruj till late hours that night. She was lost in his thoughts even while she had her dinner at the hostel mess. She was still sitting on her bed thinking of him. The feeling became too strong to be overlooked and ignored. In anxiety, she tore the pages that had 'The Summer Sunshine' in them. She still did not have the heart to throw them in the dustbin. She kept the torn pages inside her diary and placed it in her bag. Her inclination towards her weird story with a crazy desperate guy never left her in peace though.

That night, Taruj kept texting Naila till 4 am.

"Naila what's wrong?"

"Hey Miss Glass, *kyu pain maarti hai yar*? (Why do you take things so personally, dear?)"

"Let's change the agreement then. Drop the love nest idea from tomorrow. Anyhow, people are totally convinced that you are my girlfriend. No need to be in the room if it makes you so uncomfortable. Okay?"

"Miss Feminist, slept?"

"Slept or thinking about me?"

"Say something??"

"I think you have slept. See you tomorrow."

Naila had been reading all those messages, but she replied to none. She was confused about the fact as to why she was waiting for his messages throughout the night. She was also confused about why she waits for him throughout the time when she stays in the campus and more. Naila was undoubtedly enjoying his attention and his company, but was still not ready to accept or admit it, even to herself.

A week later....

It has been a few days that Taruj had seen Naila writing two stories for the annual screening. The girl was much more comfortable around him now, but was still too egoistic to ask for his help and opinion upfront. It has been just over thirty days that he had known her, but he had understood her complete psychology by then. He laughed when he observed that Naila was desperate to know his opinion, but wanted him to begin the topic. She was also considering the fact that he was an award winning creative artist himself. He was the writer of a successful drama that he had written for the cultural fest of Rendezvous when he was in his first year. Taruj was not just a man with brains, but he was also a man with unmatched creativity. Naila waited impatiently for him to understand that she needed his opinion, and finally, the guy decided not to keep her impatient anymore and asked her in the evening,

"So Miss Glass, why are you writing two stories? Don't you believe in yourself enough?"

Naila looked at him in a way that she was unwilling to share her stories with him, but he knew she was desperately dying to get his opinion. She behaved carefree to his question while the two were having coffee in the canteen. She yawned and said,

"Are you talking about the screening scripts?"

What she pretended was too obvious for anyone to guess. She was utterly delighted that he had finally started discussing something made sense to her. He laughed at her fake attitude and said,

"What else do you think you have been doing these days?"

She wasn't amused with his arrogantly hilarious tone, but she overlooked it as it was she who needed his help. She sighed as she believed that she just digested a direct insult and said,

"So, I'll consider you want to know the stories in detail."

He laughed and said,

"No, I just want to know why you are writing two stories."

His answer covered her face with pride and arrogance, and she said,

"Oh, don't give me that look Taruj."

She sounded sarcastic and he knew he had offended her. He laughed as she expressed her anger and further said,

"Don't you remember condition number three?"

He took a moment to recall the weird

conditions that she had posed in front of him in lieu of her help that she had offered him. As he was lost in his thoughts, she said,

"No need to dig your empty mind so hard. I'll help you in remembering the most important condition again."

He was amused to see her anger that was childish, full of pride and somewhat needy as well. She looked at him in frustration and said,

"You had to help me with anything I would need. It was a part of my condition number three."

He smiled and said,

"So you agree that you need my help, right?"

She opened her mouth and closed it again in smartness. She thought for fifteen minutes and finally she said,

"Well, this is not any favor from you. It is a part of the contract."

He laughed as he was finally convinced that she was too snobbish to directly accept anything from him under the tag name of 'help'. He sighed and said,

"So, you will never admit that my opinion matters to you. But you win and I lose. Yes, I want to know what the two stories are."

Naila had a winning expression on her face and she finally began as she handed over a script to him and said,

"This is the second drama, 'IIT and Life' that I have been writing for the last few days. Please have a look and let me know what do you feel about it?"

As she handed over the still incomplete script to him, he looked down at the pages and even before he could have started reading them, he said,

"Where is the first script?" He stretched his hand forward to take the script of the first drama as well, and Naila suddenly behaved weird again, and said,

"Well, that's not the script I want to focus on, you see. I need your feedback on this one."

He pulled back his hand and decided not to push her and started reading the script. It took him over an hour to complete the overall script, and in the meanwhile, Naila kept watching the changing expressions on his face. Finally, he sighed and said,

"Miss Glass, you need to know one thing before anything else."

She was eagerly waiting for a lot of praises and laurels, and had her ears open for the appreciation she was expecting. She nodded her head in agreement to show that she was listening, and he said,

"Scripts are not this long."

He miffed the girl with the first few words from his mouth. He decided to continue with his genuine feedback and further said,

"This is not even half the story and it's so lengthy already."

Naila wasn't much convinced, but he continued and said,

"You need to understand that scripts are unlike novels. You need to describe more in fewer words. That's the beauty of writing scripts, my dear."

Before he could have continued further, the little Naila with her big ego stood up in anger and said,

"Oh, I know you are a one-time champ in the creative area in your campus, but does that mean you can scrutinize even the best of works?"

He laughed as he realized she couldn't handle criticism in a healthy manner. He smiled quietly and she further said,

"You just cannot believe that someone does something better than you."

She held her bag and started walking away. He chased her outside the campus and paced up with her high speed. While running after her, he said,

"Oh, that's a lie. You have failed to handle criticism. Infact, I have not even started criticizing you. What I was telling you were just the basics of writing a good script. But you got angry in the beginning itself."

Naila turned down whatever he had to say and she continued arguing with him till he dropped her at her hostel, and even afterwards, through phone calls and messages. Finally, he gave up his will to help her craft a better script, and she continued doing what she felt was the best.

Days started passing speedily and finally, thirty days of her summer internship had gone. Taruj and Naila had been inseparable for the last one month of her summer internship at IIT Delhi. He came everyday to pick her up and came back to drop her as well. She shared a journey with him, a story that had something more to it. His desperate looks, cheap jokes and fake confidence; suddenly, Naila started seeing humor in all of it.

It was the beginning of the second month of her internship now. By that time, the awkward feeling had started to vanish away. It was a hypothetical friendship- a friendship that was accepted and valued upfront by Taruj, but totally denied by Naila. Taruj had seen Naila desperately writing a love story that she would narrate to him, but never let him read the same. She was wary of her capabilities as a romance teller.

Thus, she dropped the idea of continuing the love story and started refining her drama 'IIT and Life', as per the few instructions she had managed to hear from him, before her ego had come in between the otherwise healthy discussion that evening. Eventually, the day arrived when Naila had to narrate her script in front of the HOD of IIT's cultural fest. She turned into a storyteller and intensified her voice to do justice to the different sections of her play- 'IIT and life'. She narrated the best she could to get a positive response from the HOD and the *junta* (Students in IIT, as popularly called in the IIT lingo). Naila took an hour to complete her oration and finally, she was done.

There was still absolute silence in Auditorium number one.

Five minutes passed... then ten and then, fifteen minutes passed by.

Finally, the HOD stood up and said,

"That's all?"

Naila's heart sank as she could not see even a single pleased face around.

"Did you hear a single clap at the end till now?"

He certainly was not amused and had a horrible look on his face. Naila went into a hard shell as she spoke nothing and silently kept standing at a corner.

"The story has no base. The humor is lagging and unnatural. It's superficial and shallow. This is what you would make my team act on two months later?"

Silence...

"You've wasted thirty days and beaded a hollow script that cannot even hold emotions?"

THE LOST SUNSHINE

Silence...

"Fifteen days, and I need the first draft of the final script on my desk. Else be responsible for the remarks on your training certificate young lady. Give up writing then."

A miffed and irritated HOD of the cultural fest wing departed, leaving Naila in tears that she somehow managed to hold back. Eventually, the crowd started departing with hints of consoling comments.

"Aray koi nahi, 15 din me *firse machaate hain* (Don't worry, we'll rock it together in the next fifteen days)."

"It happens with the best of authors, just a bad day."

The voices completely flounced and Naila was still standing at the same corner- hurt and numb. She was unmoved, silent and certainly in shock. Suddenly, the voice of some faint footsteps started becoming louder and louder as someone inched closer to Naila.

"Hey, Miss Glass, it's okay."

Taruj rushed close to Naila from behind. He came

in front and as soon as he did, a tear kissed Naila's cheeks, first the left one and then the right.

"No, don't cry Naila, please don't."

He grabbed Naila in his arms and wrapped them around her gently. Moments to come were silent and had a voice of dying sobs. The warmth of his shoulders, the strength of his arms, the concern in his voice, the pain and panic he was in, seeing Naila break down- all of it conveyed a mesmerizing feeling to Naila. She was totally hooked into this guy she had met barely a month ago or so.

The intensity of his pumping heart cascaded Naila into a road of breezy and passionate romance. She held him back very closely. She wrapped her hands around his waist, dropped down her script and hid her face against his chest. Her long and open hair danced in the air and Taruj tightened his arms softy to give her all the comfort that she needed. Moments of silent romance kept dragging the two young souls closer and closer. Suddenly, Naila pushed him away and started moving out in extreme anger and disgust.

"What the hell?" She shouted loudly as she picked up her script and stormed out of the Auditorium in a rush. Taruj gave her a speedy chase and in laughter, he yelled,

"Hey, Naila please wait!"

Naila stopped for a while, gave him a cold stare and started walking away.

"Listen please!"

Taruj requested her to stop, while he was still in the moment that had just passed between the two.

"Men are dogs, literally dogs. You have just one thing in your mind, right?"

Naila was fuming as she was trying to storm away from Taruj, but he just wouldn't give up chasing her.

"Smart woman!"

He replied and still in fits of laughter, he continued,

"From day one you know I'm totally attracted to you, right? Then who asked you to grab my waist and place a soft kiss on my chest?"

He teased Naila and the girl had no rescue to deny what had happened. Though, Naila was Naila, she found a better excuse and said,

"You hugged me and I hugged you back, as friends

though."

Before Naila could have completed, Taruj interrupted and said,

"Wait a minute, come again. Am I mistaken or did the lady just say 'as friends'? This is cool, when you finally couldn't resist my charm and kissed me, you come upto me and accept that we are friends. Now don't you deny that you kissed me Naila, I just wish you had your gloss on."

Taruj's nasty comments were appealing Naila, but she was still too shrewd and adamant to accept her inclination towards a man.

"Rest your thoughts Mr. Despo. I never kissed you. I just placed my face on your chest. It's you who got your balls in between, not me." Naila replied.

"I'm a guy my dear. I'm sure you were in the moment too. But nature has its ways. There's no trap made for women to be caught like men." He still replied with a smile since he knew what the truth was.

"Oh shut up, you've broken condition number one."

Naila was certainly not ready to accept or give

in at all. He simply kept laughing and chasing Naila as she started walking towards her hostel. They took a bus to her hostel and Taruj managed to get a seat for her. While she was sitting, he said,

"So, what are you going to do now? Do you have a story?"

"I don't know." Naila replied with a blank look on her face.

"Why don't you write something that stays close to your heart? About family, college, friends or me?" He joked while giving her serious options for the script.

"And why would people want to know what my life holds?" Naila sarcastically replied while rejecting all his ideas at once.

"Write what your heart wants you to write, not what the public wants to know. When something is written from the heart, it makes its way to reach hearts." Taruj replied as he looked directly into her eyes. Naila went shy of his passionate glares and turned her face away from him, and started looking outside the window. He further said,

"You didn't let me help you with this script. Had you executed your ideas in a better way, even this script had the potential to be a huge hit."

She was still looking outside the window, but was attentive to whatever he was saying. She nodded her head in agreement and agreed that her ego spoilt her first impression. He further said,

"Wise people don't repeat the same mistakes a second time."

Naila agreed to every single word that he was saying deep inside. He further said,

"You had been writing a love story that you partially told me about. Why don't you give me the script? I'll help you craft it in a better way."

Naila was willing to take his help but something pulled her back, and she said,

"No, it's unworthy."

She turned down all his attempts to help her and days started passing by. Taruj read the tension in her mind and the deep depression that had started bothering the young girl. She would write some pieces of paper, but always end up tearing and dumping them in the dustbin.

Days after days passed away. Taruj kept reading the silence in Naila's eyes. She had a clear fear of being a complete failure. That fear was stopping her from writing anything with her heart involved. He kept giving her numerous ideas each day, she kept rejecting them all. He would see her pen down something and then tear the pages in the end. While she would dump some pages in the dustbin, she would keep some others inside a diary in her bag.

On the evening of the thirteenth day, Taruj grabbed her near the big lawn under a huge tree. She was sitting under the tree and writing something. He took her with a surprise and said,

"Show me what you are writing."

Naila covered the pages in a rush. She had sweat all over her forehead as she saw him close. She pushed him away and he laughed mysteriously. Naila was taken aback with his weird behavior (though according to her, he had behaved weird from the first day that they had met).

"What is wrong with you?"

She yelled at him as she kept holding the pages tightly in her hands and finally, she stood up. She looked down at him and said,

"I need to sit alone. I need to finish this script and

it's just half done right now. Please don't disturb me."

She started moving away with the pages in her hands when Taruj suddenly yelled and said,

"Miss Glass, your....."

As he was speaking, he decided to not continue suddenly. Naila was too occupied to notice that he had just changed some topic. He further said,

"When you feel you need to go back home, let me know. I'll be in my room. Call me and I'll come to drop you. Okay?"

She nodded her head in a yes and moved away. She worked for some hours and finally called Taruj and said,

"It's 9 pm. Please drop me back now."

Soon he reached the gate where she was waiting for him. He had her bag in his hands that he had found lying on the lawn where she was working. He had safely collected the bag and decided to not disturb her until she would have called him herself. When he reached the gate, he handed over the bag to Naila and said,

"I found it lying on the lawn. You probably dropped

it by mistake. I didn't want to disturb you while you were working. So I kept it safely."

He smiled at her as she took the bag gracefully. But she was too furious to acknowledge his smile and Taruj knew that she was stressed. She started walking with him and none of the two spoke. He dropped her safely and soon the night passed by, and the fourteenth day arrived. It was evening now. Though she had a cracking story, but it was still incomplete. On her way to the hostel, she was doomed and silent, and the guy knew it.

"What have you planned to do now?"

Taruj finally spoke after hours of silence between the two, while they were in a bus to her hostel.

"I tried my ass out to get a story, but I feel I couldn't."

Naila looked at him and further said,

"Maybe he's right. Maybe I am a shallow writer."

She looked at him and longed for some assurance. He sighed and said,

"You tried your ass out. I just wish you had tried your heart out Naila."

With this much said, Naila stood up and started getting down. Taruj gave her a chase, but before he could speak Naila said,

"I'll walk alone from here. You take a bus back to your hostel now."

She walked away and Taruj saw her disappearing with the crowd. That complete night passed away in silence. Naila's phone buzzed, but just for a few calls from the customer care and one call from her mother. It was a strange, lonely night that had come after one and half months of being with Taruj, day in and day out. It had no signs of him. His absence was clearly bothering Naila.

She grabbed her phone a number of times, typed messages again and again, but could never get over her ego and send the first text. She wanted his help this time, his genuine help. She decided to give up her ego. Finally, she gained the strength to surpass her huge ego and she called him up, but his phone was unreachable. Naila grabbed a corner of her room's window. She peeped out to see the night sky that had some stars and the moon. The moon seemed to be less pretty that night and the stars had no shine. The breeze had no sound and it was a dark, lonely and scary night. She thought to herself for a while and

THE LOST SUNSHINE

said,

"I'll present this script tomorrow. Hopefully, the HOD will give me some more time. Hopefully, it will not be as shallow as the previous one."

She assured herself, but she knew it wasn't the script that was affecting her this time, but his sudden absence. She fell asleep after 4 am in the morning and woke up jumping to a knock at her door. She looked up at the wall clock and was shocked to see it was 2 pm.

"What the hell!" She thought to herself as she hurried to get the door.

"Didi, aaj aap gae nahi? (You didn't go to your college today?)"

A small boy on the door asked Naila. He was chotu, the son of the hostel's warden. Naila smiled at him and replied,

"Nahi chotu, aaj nahi gai. Aaj to bhaiya bhi chale gae honge na wait karke? (No chotu, I couldn't get up on time today. The boy who waits for me each day must have also left after waiting, right?)"

Naila asked the little boy secretly praying that he says a yes.

"Vo bhaiya jo roz waiting room me aate hain? (The same boy who comes and waits in the waiting room daily?)" The little boy asked.

"Han (yes)." Naila replied.

"Nahi, vo to aaj aaye he nahi. (No, he did not come today)."

Chotu's reply broke Naila's heart. She couldn't think of anything that went wrong between her and Taruj.

"He did not text me nightlong. He neither came to pick me up today. What went so wrong?"

She thought to herself as she felt some pain in her throat, since she was holding back tears. Suddenly, her phone vibrated and she jumped to find out if the message was from Taruj.

"You are late!"

The message did read from Taruj, but it broke Naila's heart a little more. She saw he had texted her earlier as well. The text at 12.30 pm read,

"You have your narration lined at 1. I hope you have left."

And the second one at 2.15 pm,

"You are late!"

With a broken heart, puzzled feelings and zero enthusiasm, Naila stepped out of her hostel at 3 pm. She switched off her phone in disgust and anger. After struggling with the traffic and her broken heart, Naila managed to enter the campus of IIT Delhi at 4.30 pm. The moment she entered the gate, she looked around. It was the same campus she had been in love with for the last one and half months. But suddenly, there was nothing special about the otherwise magical campus. She walked straight to the auditorium with small steps.

"There you are!"

An annoyed HOD yelled as soon as he saw Naila.

"Don't you value people's time?"

Silence……

"Is this how you plan to work professionally?"

Silence……

This time the silence was very long. It made Naila uncomfortable. She knew she had a script, but she did not know if the HOD would find it worthy enough to have waited for it for three hours. She took a deep breath and decided to apologise and narrate the story in front of everyone again. She sighed and said,

"Sir…."

Before she could have spoken a word more, the HOD interrupted and said,

"I agree writers and creative artists are moody people. But making us wait for three hours to clap is a bad idea my dear."

The HOD finally smiled at poor Naila who was almost and already in tears. To her shock, the complete auditorium melted away in cheers, claps, laurels and smiles. She stood shocked and confused at her place.

Once the claps quieted, the HOD said,

"Wonderful work Naila."

He left the auditorium and eventually the crowd cleared up layer by layer. Every passing layer had a complement for Naila.

"*Macha dia yar* (you rocked it dear)."

"The summer sunshine rocks Miss Glass!"

"I missed your oration Miss Feminist!"

THE LOST SUNSHINE

Soon, Naila was left alone. She knew it was him, but she couldn't find out how he managed to do all this.

Suddenly, the voice of some faint footsteps started becoming louder and louder as someone inched closer to Naila once again. She closed her eyes to feel his voice and his touch once again.

"Naila, he met with an accident."

In the next moment, Naila's heart stopped beating for a minute. She couldn't relate to what she had just heard. And immediately, she turned around to face the guy. It was one of his friends, who continued,

"He's in the hospital."

Naila's happiness somehow died and she could no more feel the beating of her own heart. She rushed to the hospital with his friend. All the way to the hospital, she was numb. Her brain had stopped working at all. After half an hour, she reached a ward and there he was lying on a bed, in between the pool of fellow IITians.

"Dost he sacche hote hain bhai, teri bandi to aayi he nahi. (Brother, only friends are real, your girlfriend did not even come to see you.)"

"Pain killer ne kaam kia, ya teri bandi ko bula de? (Did the pain killer work or shall we get your girl now?)"

He was lying there with a bandage on his head and left leg. He looked weak, but still had a lot of teeth. Naila was glued to his very sight and could see no one else around him. She began to approach him slowly and the sound of giggles and laughter eventually cleared on her arrival. She had tears by then and soon, the room was left vacant with just the two of them inside.

Naila sat close to him, grabbed his hand and closed her eyes, as she cried. Suddenly, she was taken aback with a seductive voice that said,

"So the tigress started falling in love?"

A smile rested on Naila's lips as she knew that the truth was out of the box already. She looked too worried though. Before she could speak a word, he said,

"I wish I could wrap you in my arms."

He pointed out toward his hurt left shoulder and said,

"Bad luck!"

THE LOST SUNSHINE

He was still grinning to Naila's expression of concern, shock and happiness, all at the same time. She finally managed to speak and she said,

"How did you..? And this accident?"

Naila was in the spell of mixed feelings- one was of the fresh splash of first love and the other was of the pain to see him hurt. He simply smiled at her and said,

"I used to collect all the pages you used to dump in the dustbin. You never realized that I was genuinely trying to help you to make a successful script this time. But the pages you were dumping one after the other, barely revealed the story to me. I tried hard to imagine the concept but couldn't, until the day you left your bag in the lawn by mistake."

Naila was silent as she remembered that the day before yesterday, he had handed over her bag to her near the gate of the IIT campus. She smiled absurdly and said,

"And you were behaving so decent at that point of time. Like you actually found the bag lying and did not steal it."

He grinned and said,

"For a moment, I was going to inform you when I called you, but then I realized, I could actually steal your bag for some time. You were too occupied to realize that I changed the topic."

She suddenly interrupted him and said,

"But still, how did you do all this? And how did this accident happen?"

He took a deep sigh and said,

"You never looked back yesterday. I had the plan to help you. I wanted to surprise you. I was totally lost in your fragrance. I took the bus back to IIT, but close to the main gate a car hit me from the back. I was too lost in your spell. I hardly saw the car coming in speed. I opened my eyes in the hospital late at night and all that I remembered for a few moments was your face."

    Taruj remained quiet for a while. It was airy and Naila's long, un-clutched hair played around her face and those big eyes of hers behind the thick round glasses. He lifted himself up to sit and tilted close to Naila. He raised his right hand and placed his palm gently on her face. Naila was in the moment as she closed her eyes to feel his touch. Taruj gently worked away some of those hair from her eyes and said,

"Hey Miss Glass, I love your eyes. You are going to kill me someday."

Suddenly, a cool gust of storm banged the windows of Naila's room. Tara and Naila were taken aback with the entry of a storm that had started getting stronger. The two came back to their senses and Naila realized she had started living her forgotten past all over again. Tara had wet eyes and a choking voice by then, to see Naila fall in love with him once more. The poor girl looked outside and said,

"There's no moon, there's no star. Is it his absence from my life, my forgotten memories or a painful destiny, that I am falling in love with a man for whom my soul craves, mother?"

Tara had no relief that she could have offered to the aching soul of her poor daughter.

"I want to know this man, mother. I want to know what more did the air of 2009 had for me. I dreamt of his first voice that night. I saw a hospital ward in the dream. The shadows of a man and a woman were me and him soon after his accident. Maybe, it was the very first time that he had said,

"Hey Miss Glass, I love your eyes. You are going to kill me someday." She deeply sighed and further said,

"And I exactly want to know how I killed him at last."

Tara realized Naila had herself to blame for the pain she was going through. A pain of the departure of a man Naila did not even remember, a man who gave up his life for hers, but was still a mystery.

"What happened then, mother?"

Naila's big eyes had gone teary and her mother began again,

"You and he were captivated in a lifetime sentence of a soulful romance. The feelings between the two of you were fresh, and passion kept dragging you both closer and closer."

Naila soon drowned in the memories of her forgotten love and her soul landed somewhere in the mists of 2009, when they both shared their first confession of love.

"Hey Miss Glass, I love your eyes. You are going to kill me someday."

THE LOST SUNSHINE

Taruj was captivated in the moment of his first expression of love to Naila. He gently placed his right hand against her waist and pulled her close. He was looking straight in Naila's eyes and shyly, she moved away from him. He laid back on the bed. He was smiling to himself, and finally, he spoke up and said,

"How did you not notice the missing diary and the pages of your script from the bag?"

She was lost in his essence and she said,

"The pages were not fair. I had written things over and over again. And I was too worried to notice that you had stolen my diary."

He grinned and further said,

"You have no idea, those pages revealed to me the story that the dumped pages in the dustbin could not."

Naila grew shy and he paused for a while, smiled to himself, and said,

"I always wanted to steal your bag, you know."

He giggled notoriously and Naila watched him impatiently as he further spoke,

"Once I reached my love nest the day before yesterday, I checked your bag. There was a diary and something else too."

The devilish tease in his eyes broadened and he nastily said,

"Who keeps a collection of Bra tags in the bag?"

Naila was silent and he burst into a loud laughter.

"Now I know what size you are."

He winked at Naila and she yelled,

"You bastard, how dare you?"

She stood up in anger and was going to leave when Taruj slowly grabbed her hand and calmed her down. He placed his finger on her lips and said,

"I would never reveal what I saw in your bag to anyone. I promise."

Somehow Naila was hooked into the very sight of this weird, yet incredibly handsome, man. He had been underrating his looks in the real deficiency of women in his campus though. Totally humorous but damn poking, a big time desperate but soft and witty- that was this guy from IIT who had made a huge impact on the little Miss feminist Naila.

He continued and Naila was totally blown away with his charisma. He further said,

"After inspecting your bag in the love nest for over an hour, I needed a serious break for the guy thing." He smiled and said,

"It was a serious offense to your condition number one though."

Naila was growing shy of his looks, his voice and even his face. He continued,

"After having done with the guy thing, I opened up the diary. Some pages fell down. I collected all of them and placed them on my bed. Some of them were torn to two pieces and some others were torn to four, but some were just fine."

He took a moment of silence and further continued,

"I taped down the torn papers and arranged them with numbers you had given on top and bottom of each page. And my heart stopped beating for a while."

The two remained absolutely silent. Taruj and Naila, they both were looking at each other, and he said while looking straight in her eyes,

"I found my story written on those pages. 'The Summer Sunshine' it was."

As he became quiet, silence intoxicated Naila's soul as she somehow knew that she was in love with this man. He said,

"It was you and me. The tigress secretly kept beading us in words. You turned my world upside down for those hours when I read your incomplete script Naila."

He smiled at her and said,

"It was a welcome trip to my past one and half months that reminded me of hanging around this little feminist angry girl, who hated being dated."

He laughed to himself and said,

"I started completing your script as I exactly knew what was going to happen in the plot next. I exactly knew the places where you had struggled. By the time I fell asleep; most of it was done, but still needed a final touch up."

He took a pause for a while, as it seemed that the two were sharing secret sessions of falling in love. He sighed and further said,

"The next day when I dropped you back to the

hostel, I was absolutely sure that I will surprise you with the complete script the next morning. But my accident killed a lot of time. When I woke up in the ward, I asked one of my friends to get your diary and the script I had mostly written from my room. I completed the script last night in the ward. But I did not want you to know about it so casually. That's when I switched off my phone and left you guessing about my sudden absence from your life. I wanted to give you time to realize that your life is as empty without me, as mine is without you.

I handed over the script to my friend and asked him to hand it over to you when you would arrive at the campus. You had your narration at 1. But you did not show up on time. When the HOD was planning to screw you, my friend handed over the script to him. He said that you were unwell and that you had handed over the script to him in case you get late the next day. The angry HOD narrated the story out loud with a motto to insult you, but by the end of it, he and everyone else fell in love with your story. 'The Summer Sunshine' was out. The HOD was so impressed that he decided to wait for you."

Naila was stunned and she knew that she was blessed with a man like him. He further said,

"Once you arrived and the crowd cleared, my friend told you about my accident. I did not want to spoil your moment of victory with this news." He was deeply in love with Naila- the girl who had turned his world upside down. He laughed loudly, and further said,

"I have loved flirting with women of all ages, shapes and sizes, but this time it was the best- flirting with a woman who hated............."

As he was going to complete his words, Naila moved close to him on the bed and in the heat of running emotions, she kissed him.

Once she released him from her magic spell, she said,

"You speak a lot and I hate it."

"Let me know what you love then, I'd love to do it for you."

With this much said, Taruj pulled Naila very close. He played with her flowing hair and kept looking in her eyes, till she shyly turned them down. He gently placed his right hand around Naila's waist. The two young, freshly in love duo, sank in the ocean of unheard romance and passion.

THE LOST SUNSHINE

"Now, that's how you kiss Miss Glass..."

Said Taruj and he kissed Naila. For moments, the two remained lost in the heat of passion. After sometime, Naila opened her eyes and in confusion and nervousness, she pulled herself away from Taruj, and said while stammering,

"Now, don't go too far in your dirty mind."

He simply laughed, looking at her confusion as she further said,

"I kissed you to say thank you."

She hurriedly stood up and started running away. Before leaving the ward, she turned back and smiled at Taruj. She said,

"I hope you'll come to drop me back to the hostel once you are well again. I will come to see you daily Mr. Despo."

Naila quickly moved away, smiling, and left back a lost and totally in love 'Taruj'. Time flew with wings on it and after fifteen days, he was fine again. Naila was exceedingly happy to find him around in the campus that had no fun in his absence. She headed her way straight to the canteen that evening to greet him, soon after he was discharged. As she entered, she could see Taruj surrounded by a thick crowd of men. On getting closer, she heard,

"The Summer Sunshine, let us know all the details brother."

"We need the details of what happened in the hospital ward too."

Such comments brought Naila back to the reality. She collected a hint of tears and left the place. She was slowly moving close to the main gate. Suddenly, she realized that Taruj has given her a chase. She ignored his callings and fastened her steps to keep away from him.

"Naila, hey!"

Finally, he managed to grab her and pull her near the tree that stood close to the main campus gate.

"Hey, what's wrong?"

He said with extreme concern, as he tried to wipe a tear off Naila's face. She abruptly pushed away his hand, and replied while sobbing,

"So now you are going to give away these details too?"

THE LOST SUNSHINE

He simply smiled at her anger and said,

"If you heard all this, you must have also noticed that I gave away no detail."

He stood silent to get Naila's response. She stood silent so he continued,

"They are my friends Naila. It is not exactly the way you think it is. We joke around, since we have all been like a family for years now. They are not what you think they are. I am not what you thought I was."

She was still silent and unmoved. He held her hand in his and said,

"We both were not even friends then. You insisted you are my hypothetical girlfriend. How could I....."

Before he could have completed, Naila interrupted and said,

"You wouldn't have done what you have been doing, had I been your real girlfriend?"

"Doing what?" He replied calmly.

"Talking shit behind my back to prove that you are a natural in luring women."

He smiled at her and said,

"I wouldn't have had the need to show that I am a natural, had you actually been my girlfriend. I faked just to show off. But you are no more a hypothetical myth in my life."

Silence marked an awkward moment between the two. Taruj finally said,

"Now, you are my summer sunshine."

He looked in her eyes yet again and said,

"Oh, I love your eyes, love."

He gently brushed his lips against hers. The two had fallen in love irrevocably and unconditionally. He took her back to the canteen and said,

"So, what would you like to have maam?"

"What's the menu?" Naila smilingly replied.

"It's tea, coffee and cutlets in veg. and Taruj Singh in non-veg."

Naila rose from her seat and said,

"I like the non-veg. menu more."

The seduction in her voice and the warmth in her

smile enchanted Taruj as the newly-in-love couple headed its way to the love nest. The room was still a mess. It was still clustered by a huge crowd that chased the two. Nothing seemed to be bothering Naila anymore. She sat down on the bed and said,

"So, you've got the playboy posters back again?"

"I'll take them off if you say so." He replied passionately.

Naila pulled him close and said,

"Don't get your balls in between. I hate it."

"They have always been at the correct place and time." He replied as he placed a kiss on Naila's neck. As she started getting cozy, he took a deep sigh and pulled himself back and said,

"Okay, let's be friends first. I need you to know that I will never be your dad before anything else." Naila was stunned as he continued,

"I read your diary, remember? I know what scared you in men and why you were hostile to fall in love." Naila stood up smiling, and said,

"I already know this."

He smiled at her and stretched his hand forward

for a handshake, and said,

"Friends then?"

She grabbed his hand and said,

"Well, kissing is more hygienic than handshakes."

Taruj laughed at her innocent love plays and kissed her passionately.

Moments later, he said,

"Now that I took what you said, you would come upto me and say, sex is more hygienic than kissing. Would that mean I should have sex with you?"

A cool breeze intoxicated Naila's soul and she hugged him tightly and said,

"Yes."

The two young hearts slipped in passion and made love. His guy thing, their heated up in-love voices and an epic romance filled a night that they both shared for a lifetime. The coming next month, the final month of Naila's internship, strengthened her relationship with Taruj. He shared a sparking chemistry with her now- so sparking and strong that it left no mind guessing about their status and serious commitment. She spent her time preparing for the annual screenplay of 'The Summer Sunshine' in the last month of her internship at the magical campus of IIT Delhi. And he spent his time falling in love with her again and again. Soon, a month flew by and 'The Summer Sunshine' became a smashing hit, and Naila and Taruj became a popular story in the campus forever.

Suddenly, the voices of birds and mild breeze reminded Tara of the reality and she realized it was 5 am. She looked at Naila who had her eyes closed, and was smiling.

"Mother, I feel like I know this man." Naila said, still smiling, with her eyes closed.

"Sure you do Naila. You both were inseparable until his…"

The awkward silence made Naila gain back her senses and she said,

"I regret not knowing his face despite he touched my soul once."

Her eyes were gloomy to the thought that her recent love would never find her back again.

"He might be gone from your life and your memories, but he still stays to be your true love."

Tara smiled at Naila and continued,

"There's much more to this story. But it's too late now. Rest for now and I'll let you take a dive in the ocean of love yet again."

Tara kissed her daughter and left the room.

Naila kept looking at the letter that marked the presence of this mystery man in her life.

"You always found me in life. Why can't you find me back again?"

Her innocent eyes had pain of not being able to see him, feel him, touch him and love him.

"What would it have been being in love with you, when losing you without knowing you is so tough?" She looked at the letter she was hugging and kissed it.

"I pray I feel your touch once again, Mr. Despo."

A tear rolled down her eyes, and she sobbed in silence till she fell asleep that morning.

CHAPTER FIVE

MY LOVE...FOR YOU

For hours to come and go, Naila tried hard to remember his face, to remember how he smiled and what his touch felt like, but it was all in vain. She searched every possible corner of her brain to revive the old dead memories of being in love with a dead man, but all she was left with was a severe pain in her head and also her heart.

"Naila, stop exerting your brain please. I said I will eventually let you know the complete truth each night. You will kill yourself this way."

Tara told Naila as she gave her a medicine for the headache that had gone out of control. Naila was quiet as she saw that her mother was growing furious. She tried to put Naila to sleep and left the room only after the girl faked sleeping. Naila was still awake, and Taruj's absence and the absence of his memories were depressing her.

"Hello Doctor Arora, its Tara, Naila's Mother."

Tara had called up Naila's doctor to let him know about her headache.

"Oh hello Mrs. Joshi, I hope Naila is doing just fine with the story so far." The doctor asked in concern.

"Well, I suppose she did until this morning though. She has been complaining of a terrible headache which I suspect has resulted because of her trying too hard to remember Taruj's face." Tara worriedly told the doctor and waited for his response.

"Then why are you keeping her guessing? Show her a picture of his and then she'll stop scanning her lost memory to find out what he looked like."

Tara kept the phone after a reassurance from the doctor that Naila was still managing her forgotten past quite well. She scanned every inch of her closet to discover a picture of Taruj. She found one of her favorites from the summers of 2011. Tara developed tears in her eyes, remembering the happy times when they both, Taruj and Naila, were together. She got a hold of her emotions and entered Naila's room with some pictures hidden in her hands.

THE LOST SUNSHINE

"Naila, how do you feel now, my child?"

Tara seemed to have broken a spell Naila was captured into, and the girl said,

"Mother, I see his shadows and hear his voice. I can't see it clear though."

Naila had developed sweat all over her forehead, as she was trying way too hard to dig her gone and forgotten memories in order to find out how her love in the past looked like.

"Relax, my child. You want to know how he looked like, right?"

Tara just eased Naila a little and the girl said,

"Yes mother."

Tara smiled at her daughter and said,

"Well, I'll help you with it and I promise you would soon know what he looked like and what it felt like being around him."

Naila had a deep satisfaction in her heart now that soon, she would get to know how the mystery man Taruj exactly looked.

Tara started to unveil the story further,

"Taruj and you fell into the hands of a passionate romance. You used to take out time from the busy spells in your life and inform me about how different a man could be from what your father was. I was extremely happy, since I had never seen you so comfortable with anyone else in life other than me. I was assured that if someone could take care of you after me, it would be him. And I wasn't wrong in any way. He valued your life and happiness way above his own. Taruj and you spent a year of being inseparable, and finally, he got a placement at some company in Mumbai when he was in the fourth year of his course. You were unsure of his decision to grab that opportunity, as you were worried of losing your precious relationship with him towards the end of 2010."

Naila drowned in what her mother narrated and her heart raced back to the faint memories of the winters of 2010, which had another soul soaking love plunge hidden in its garb.

"Naila, please trust me. I will never change and will always love you."

Taruj tried to convince Naila over a lunch date on the 13th of December, 2010.

"That's what most men say when they are over and

tired of a single girl." Naila replied as she pretended to concentrate completely on the juice she had ordered.

"That happens with men who date one woman. You are a bunch of various Nailas' residing in your single lean body, you know that?" Taruj joked and Naila replied,

"Is that supposed to be funny?"

She was sarcastically tough to be handled when she framed an opinion about a certain thing.

"Listen baby, are you still unsure of my love for you?" Taruj assertively asked hoping that she would say a no.

"Yes."

Naila replied only to drop down his shoulders. He sighed and said,

"What more do I have to say if you still don't trust me enough Naila." He was hurt and Naila realized it. She kept her hand on his and said,

"Everyone back at my college says that long distance relationships never work out. Take me with you or just stay back with me, please."

She pleaded him like a small child and he said,

"I would have loved to take you with me. But baby, you have your studies. Just complete your course and then look around for a job in Mumbai." Naila looked down on the table for some minutes and then said,

"I would have done that but my mother might not allow me to move to Mumbai. The city is too far from my hometown." Naila was doomed and gloomy to the very thought of being away from her man for around one and half years, that's when her course would have actually ended.

"So, should I turn down this job offer and look around for other jobs in Delhi only?"

Naila knew he meant every bit of the options he ever gave. Hence she said,

"No. I know how dearly you want to make a switch to this job and your dream city."

"I need you to have faith in love, have faith in me, Naila. We'll not end up parting ways like most of the couples do. I will never let you down, my darling. I will never leave you alone." Taruj assured Naila and she said,

THE LOST SUNSHINE

"You promise?"

He smiled back at her innocent eyes and said,

"I promise."

"So, when do you plan to make a shift to Mumbai?" Naila asked Taruj after getting some assurance from him.

"In July next year, baby." He replied.

"So, I want you to meet Tara, my mother, before you shift to Mumbai, if that's not an issue?"

Naila looked for his assurance and he said,

"Sure I will, not an issue."

Time started flowing at a brisk pace and soon it was June 2011. Taruj had planned a holiday for Naila at Udaipur, before he would have shifted to Mumbai. He took her out for a dinner date one day and said,

"So, it's June now and in a month's time, I'll be shifting to Mumbai." Naila was silent as he continued speaking further,

"I am taking you out on a secret vacation, my queen. Get your mom alongside and spoil the fun."

He grinned as Naila stared back at him. She overlooked his nasty joke and said,

"Where are we going then, and when?"

Naila's eyes glittered with the joy of a secret long vacation with Taruj. She was also excited for the fact that she would make the two most important people in her life to greet each other for the first time in reality. As Naila continued to chirp away, Taruj placed his hand on his heart and said,

"Oh your eyes Naila, you will surely kill me someday. I love you so much."

He sighed deeply and Naila laughed at his weird love expressions. He smiled at Naila and said,

"Oh, I wish it was as easy for me to cover up as it is for you."

"You can't resist dragging your boy thing in between?" Naila joked as she knew what exactly he meant.

"I still have a secret crush on you even after being with you for almost two years now." Taruj replied only to make Naila a little shyer.

"So, where are we going for the vacation?" She changed the topic completely.

"Udaipur!" Taruj replied while gazing at Naila's radiant smile.

Naila's eyes were filled with royal romance, thinking of the princely city with the legends of great kings and rulers. She said,

"Good then. I'll ask Tara to drop in on the second day of our trip. Okay?"

"Why the second day? What do you plan to do on the first day then?" He got a hint of seduction to his voice and the two merrily fought in arguments and made up easily.

A week past his dinner date with Naila, Taruj took her to a romantic vacation at Udaipur. The city was too welcoming. The folklores, royal romance, cultural touch and smell of bravery added slight mystery to the romantically royal city of Udaipur- the royal city with majestic lakes.

'Rang Mahal Palace' was a fascinating resort and Naila's adventure home for the next seven days to come. The resort had hymns of royal tales encrypted all over. It was also a property of great heritage value. It was a beautiful heritage property that had a pool bar as well. The front side of that pool bar had stone chairs. The guests could dip

their feet in the cool, clear, blue water of that huge pool. Traditional Rajasthani cuisines were served in the traditional 'Haveli' restaurant of that beautiful palace hotel. The Haveli Restaurant was an open air, roof top restaurant, that offered the spectacular view of the Lake Pichola and the City Palace.

Multiple international cuisines could be enjoyed in the remaining three restaurants- 'The Dhola Ghat', 'The Maru Mehal' and 'The Rajput Garh'. The morning breakfast was daily followed with the cultural oration of the *Dhola-Maru* love story, which love dipped all the guests in the palace. Dhola and Maru is a popular Rajasthani love folklore that rests in the historical pages of the Rajasthani culture. The palace had three swimming pools and sun decks in abundance for guests who loved getting sun soaked. Some majestic rooms had personal pools and private Jaccuzi's as well. Certainly, Naila had never been to such a majestic palace hotel ever before in her life. She loved that magical palace, and was absolutely in love with the scenic beauty of Udaipur as well. The rooms that Taruj had booked had a personal Jaccuzi and also offered a view of the gigantic Pichola Lake. A fascinating cool breeze from the castle-type windows of that royal room made the ambience lively and romantic.

"Had I been the king, you would still have been my favorite queen, Naila."

Taruj joked as he soon started to get the fits of royalty in that amazing resort.

"Had I been your favorite queen, I would have killed all the other queens, my prince charming."

Naila joked back, but had hints of jealously hidden.

"Why would you have killed them all? After all, royalty needs endless options for romance and love."

Taruj joked only to arouse the jealousy in Naila. He loved it when she turned jealous. He found her prettier than ever before, when she fumed after getting jealous.

"Love needs no options. True love needs no options. How would a big time desperate know that?"

Naila replied as she went angry and rolled her eyes. Before she could have said even a word more, Taruj grabbed her and pulled her close. He gave her a long kiss and said,

"You'll kill me someday with the magic of your eyes."

"Don't change the topic now." Naila said assertively, yet shyly, while breathing heavily. She gently pulled herself away from him. Taruj again pulled her close, took off her specs and said,

"You are so warm, my love."

He kissed her eyes and could feel the warm splash of her heavy breath all over his face. He pressed his lips tight against her cheeks only to make her breathe heavier. He brushed his lips on her chin and finally placed a gentle kiss on her lips. A few moments of heated up romance were followed with long hours of togetherness, as the two were lost in time and passion. Taruj gently kept his lips on Naila's neck and before kissing, he said,

"Had I been the king, you would have been my only queen."

The two finally slipped in romance and made love. It was afternoon when Taruj gently woke up Naila and said,

"Let's move out sleepy head. Let me show you some awesome places like a free bird until your mother arrives tomorrow." He grinned as he knew his jokes irritated Naila. He loved it somehow.

"Get ready, it's time to explore Udaipur."

Taruj absolutely adored Naila like a princess and his most precious belonging. He was a dream that most women want, but very few lucky ones have. He was in love with the different ladies that rested in one Naila. He loved the mysterious Naila, the detective Naila, the explorer Naila, the independent Naila and so on, the list was long.

After having lunch at the resort, Taruj hired a cab and straight away made his way to *'Haldi Ghati'*. The place holds a great historic value and Naila asked,

"So, what's so strikingly special about Haldi Ghati? We could have explored the city palace and the monsoon palace first?"

"Well maam, a friend of mine said that it's an awesome museum with..."

Before he could have completed, Naila interrupted and said,

"What? A museum! You went straight for a museum despite knowing how much I hate them?"

She was annoyed and she distanced herself to the other end of the cab. Taruj smiled at her anger and gently pulled her back.

"My little Miss Eager, if you remember, your dear diary revealed many secrets to me almost two years ago." He just made Naila impatient and curious. But before she could speak, he said,

"Well, Miss curious, the bag had a diary. Though, my favorite thing still remains to be the tag collection."

He joked as Naila simply smiled and slapped him softly, and said,

"Behave and speak up."

He smiled back at Naila and said,

"So, the diary revealed to me that your mother is a great fan of museums. It also revealed to me that, while your mother is not atypical *Garhwali* woman, she speaks Garhwali when she is hugely irritated with something or someone." He paused for a while as he saw a confusing expression on Naila's face. After the pause, he said,

"So my little Miss Confused, I just wanted to make sure that I impress her with my skills. And that can happen better if I explore the place first and then be a guide to her."

Naila was certainly impressed with his learning skills and she said,

"So, do you keep a note of all the things you learn about pretty girls or is this something special?"

"Well this is certainly something special." He confessed as he again miffed Naila with his boy thing creeping up its head again.

"You are impossible." She yelled and the two continued talking endlessly throughout the two hours long journey to Haldi Ghati. It was a journey back to history. The streets were magical. They were typical of what a person imagines when he thinks of Rajasthan in specific. It wasn't exactly sandy though, but had no shops, houses, hotels, motels, restaurants or even public toilets anywhere throughout their two hour drive. It was a typical village road that was barren and had thorny trees planted on both sides of the road. The sun was shining at its best, but the AC in their car comforted the two throughout. The rocky large boulders sometimes gave a feel of being in the land of the great warrior King Maharana Pratap.

Finally, an epic drive to the land of a great ruler's sacrifice came to an end, and they reached the museum. The entrance was carved on the top of a broad and steep road. It had a huge gate. When they entered the museum, they were hugely impressed with a gigantic statue of Maharana Pratap and his beloved horse Chetak from the war scene of the famous war of Haldi Ghati. They looked around and found numerous statues of Maharana Pratap and Chetak all around the place. It seemed that the great, kind king surely shared true love with his great friend and companion of wars- Chetak the horse. Taruj explored the counter for tickets and soon the two were taken into a small room-theatre with a few other tourists. The theatre played an animation movie about the bravery of Maharana Pratap and Chetak, and also the heroism involved in the biggest battle of its age- the Haldi Ghati War.

Taruj and Naila were drenched in patriotism by the end of that movie, that displayed the various scarifies that Maharana had done in his lifetime to nurture a true king's life. It also portrayed the fact that love needs no language. The sacrifice made by Chetak of giving up his own life to save that of his master's, was a token of special flavor in the otherwise tale of heroism, patriotism and bravery.

THE LOST SUNSHINE

The tourists were then guided through different chambers that depicted the struggles and life of Maharana Pratap despite being a ruler, through an amazing light and sound show. The show highlighted Maharana's life from his childhood to his death. The amazing time that they spent at the museum was followed by a short visit to a nearby village that was famous for its handmade drinks and goodies. They also visited *'Rakt Talai'*, which was a garden. It was built on the same ground on which the war of Haldi Ghati took place. A flowing monsoon river had turned into a river of blood with the massacre that the war had seen. The garden derived its name from the history of a bloody massacre that had taken place in one of the freedom stories of Ancient India, where a ruler disagreed to keep his land and people captive under the Great Mughal Emperor- Akbar. It was built as a token of respect to the brave soldiers who had shed their blood in the war of Haldi Ghati.

A happening yet tiring journey came to an end, and Taruj and Naila reached the 'Rang Mahal Palace'.

"So my queen, how do you rate the museum?"

Taruj asked, as he offered Naila a seat on the dinner table at the resort's restaurant.

"Quite interesting." She replied. The two had food and quietly, they slipped into the shade of a romantic night.

Early morning greeted Naila and Taruj with chirps of birds and hints of local music and folklores in the air. It was 10 am, and Taruj and Naila waited for Tara to arrive. Finally, an hour long wait ended and a slim, short lady entered the resort.

"Who else could have been the mother of this little girl?" Taruj thought to himself as he could see how alike Naila and her mother were. Naila formally introduced Tara and Taruj. She was extremely happy as she saw her mother and Taruj gelling together quite nicely. Soon, Taruj made Tara equally fond of him, and Naila said,

"What's so magical in you?"

He simply smiled and said,

"It's your love, my dear."

Soon, Taruj took Naila and her mother to explore the Haldi Ghati Museum and other local attractions in Udaipur.

"Next time, we'll plan trips in season." Naila said as she felt the heat of being in Rajasthan during the summer season.

"Then make sure you make an equal contribution to the trip as well." Tara replied before Taruj could have answered. Naila was certainly tired, but very amused to see her mother defend him so promptly.

"Oh, I will. Let me finish my studies and get a job. It's better to burn a few bucks than burning my pretty skin." Naila grinned only to leave her mother in a bit of fury. Time started passing and soon they began to reach almost the end of their trip. Taruj stole Naila for sometime while Tara was sleeping in the resort on the fifth evening of their trip. The two were having a good time, when suddenly, a voice took them with a surprise,

"Smile….."

Tara took the two young love birds by surprise and could capture a rather intense, passionate and in-love picture of the two- a picture she treasured for the rest of her life.

"Oh mom, give us a warning atleast."

Naila complained and Tara replied,

"Esan ki karan lagiracho, ki Chetavni zarurat padi

raich? (What are you doing as such that you need a warning first?)"

Taruj burst into a secret laughter as Naila looked back at him, and they realized it miffed Naila's mother.

"*Ish Kuch na Karyo, just manners ma*. (We didn't do anything as such mother, it's just about manners."

Taruj found it exceptionally humorous to see Naila talk in Garhwali, but he controlled the fits of laughter. The time passed gradually and the three (Naila, her mother and Taruj) explored every corner of the historic city of Udaipur. Tara and Taruj bonded high time in those seven days and Naila's eyes kept drooping out every single time she saw them giving each other a high five.

"What have you done to my mother?" Naila joked and Taruj replied,

"She's just like you. I feel no difference or uncomfortable in her company as well. I conquered your mother's heart. Now it's your turn to bribe me with a sweet dish tonight."

Taruj just made Naila shy on the last evening of their trip to Udaipur. The next morning, Taruj woke up and took Naila and Tara for a surprise breakfast by the sundeck of the resort's pool. He made the departure a little more special for the two ladies. After having breakfast, the three packed their bags for the checkout. Taruj secretly stole his lady love for few private moments. Naila yelled at him in whispers and said,

"What are you doing? She'll kill you." He giggled and said,

"I don't mind being killed if the stakes are a few kisses."

He gave Naila a long goodbye kiss. The girl came back to her senses moments later, and said,

"*Ki karan lagiracho tumun*? (What are you trying to do?)"

The two burst into laughter as they realized the risk involved.

"You are so like your mother, really."

Taruj sat down on his knees and held Naila's hand and said,

"I promise to be the same until my last breath."

From nowhere, Tara entered the scene with her camera and said,

"Smile…."

She snapped a memorable picture of the two and the three departed after a fun filled and loving vacation at Udaipur- one of Naila's favorite destinations now.

A cool breeze greeted Naila and Tara and the ladies realized it was 8 pm. Naila was looking straight in her mother's eyes and she said,

"How did things change so much then?"

Silence…

"We were supposed to be in so much love. You liked him too. How did he die?"

Naila had endless questions in her wet eyes. She was falling in intense love with this guy whom she was seeing in shadows and now in shadowed dreams for the past few weeks.

"Why have you changed from what you have been telling me you were?"

Naila was very deeply sad to the fact that things had changed and she still remembered nothing about her beautiful past.

"Do you see any new memory in glimpses from the

past?"

Tara coerced Naila in curiosity as she wanted her daughter's forgotten memory to resume. Naila closed her eyes for a few minutes and opened them in disgust and said,

"It's blank and black. I see nothing."

She was very annoyed and then she requested her mother,

"You have to tell me from the beginning till the end. I want to know more about him and me, mother."

Tara realized the girl's memory still could not get pictures of anything from the past without her help. She said,

"I can tell you everything except one thing that is a mystery to me as well."

"And what is that, mother?" Naila asked in surprise.

"I can let you know the details of your past till the 10th of august, 2013. None of us know the complete truth about the 11th of August of the same year. The forgotten memories either lay with you or him."

Tara stood up as tears kissed her cheeks. She fastened her hands to grab two pictures from the corner of the bed.

"Take a look Naila. It holds the closest memory of yours and the man who loved you like no one else could."

Tara handed over two pictures to Naila and left the room.

The girl shyly grabbed one of the pictures and slowly got it near her face. It was of a man, who they said was her soulmate- Taruj.

Her eyes went shy to his very sight, as the first picture revealed the surprise they were taken with when Tara entered the room without a warning. Naila was visited with the first memory of the incident from the past. She could remember the faint words of the events in a palace like room. She closed her eyes to reveal his face further clearly and there he stood in her memories. She could clearly see his smile and she burst into a painful loud cry and yelled,

"Come back Taruj. Please come back."

Tara rushed into the room, hearing a loud cry and held back the sobbing and screaming Naila,

THE LOST SUNSHINE

"Naila, what happened? Naila?"

"Mother, I saw his clear face, his smile and felt his touch. I got a glimpse of my first memory from this picture. I saw a palace like room. I need him back mother. I need him back."

Naila cried loudly in pain. Tara calmed her down and said,

"He lives in your soul, my dear."

She was happy that Naila finally started seeing clear bits from the memories she had forgotten completely.

"What else do you see, darling? Try to explore your memories a little more."

Tara was ashamed of asking her daughter to dip in a pool of pain yet again, but she knew that it was important for her to explore her memories in order to begin her life normally once again.

Naila looked at the second picture Tara gave her. The picture was of the same guy, kneeling down and holding Naila's hand. She said,

"Is it the same picture you took in the resort when he promised me that he will be the same until his last...?"

Naila could not complete her words as her voice choked.

"Yes, it is."

Tara hugged her daughter who was crying in pain.

"Please bring him back to me. I might not know his story with me without your help, but his presence and the thought of his presence removes my emptiness. I need him mother. I need him."

Naila silently cried in the arms of her mother and her heart ached for the warmth of those two strong shoulders, that once in life gave her strength, divinity, peace and love. Tara had to rush out to make dinner due to irritated spells of screams from her husband,

"Do I have to sleep empty stomach for the drama that has started happening day in and day out?"

He seemed least interested in Naila's life and her pains. As Tara was leaving the room, Naila said,

"Are you sure he's my father?"

Tara laughed as a tear rolled down her eyes.

"This is why I say that he lives in you. That's his humor you just revealed."

THE LOST SUNSHINE

She left the room and Naila closed her eyes, keeping the pictures very close to her heart.

"If you ever loved me the way she says and the way I believe you did, if you ever wanted my happiness above yours, if we ever had a special love that others don't have, come back to me."

Naila was surprisingly greeted with a cool breeze that entered the room suddenly. She responded to the rising cold and said,

"Your feel does not satisfy me anymore. If you ever loved me for real, come back and hold me once again."

A tear dropped down her eyes as she saw the picture in which he proposed to her.

That night Tara decided not to strain Naila's mind further. With a lot of patience, she succeeded in convincing Naila that she would depict the rest of the story the next morning. Tara left the room and Naila sat close to her window. She spent a few hours talking to the wind and commanding it to drop her to the place where her love was.

She fell asleep and that night, she dreamt of him again. It was a clear dream and not like the past ones in shadows. She saw him standing in his trademark style, with his hands behind his head, carrying a smile on his face and his legs crossed.

Naila woke up the next morning with her breath intoxicated with love and passion. Her heart was yearning to feel his touch once again. Her eyes had gone red in his wait, the wait that could never end throughout her life. She sat on her bed, held the pictures she was left with and cried.

"Come back to me my love, come back!"

CHAPTER SIX

THE LOST SUNSHINE

Naila spent the entire morning dipped in the memories of his clear face that she saw in her dream. Tara got busy in the kitchen work that she wanted to complete as fast as she could to help Naila recover a few more bits from her past. Naila spent most of her time by reading the letter she had discovered in her mother's closet, and by looking at the two pictures that her mother had handed over to her the previous night. It was 3 pm when finally, Tara managed to complete all her work. She entered the room and saw Naila sitting by the side of her window. She was silent, not crying, but sad.

"What's up my brave girl?"

Tara greeted Naila and placed a kiss on her forehead.

"I have tried so hard to remember all of it on my

own. But I see only that much that you have told me." Naila was clearly sad about the fact that she still couldn't remember the complete story on her own.

"But you see his face clearly now. That's a good sign dear."

Tara assured her daughter that very soon, she would remember her past clearly, without anyone's help.

"So mother, what happened between us after that Udaipur vacation ended?"

Naila was deeply indulged in the priceless, but forgotten memories of her past. Tara smiled to her and said,

"It was the beginning of a testing time in your relationship with him. For the first time, you both were going through separation, ever since you both had met. It was a long distance relationship, a relationship which is mostly discarded by the youth of your age."

Naila kept looking at her mother as she continued,

"It was the middle of the year 2012. He left for Mumbai in the second week of July after spending some more quality time with you in Delhi. Neither of you were happy with the pain that separation had caused, but you had to accept it for your careers."

Soon Naila and Tara drowned deep in the memory lane, and the story began.

Being in almost two years of an inseparable courtship, Taruj and Naila's relationship had entered a new phase- The Email Love. The very idea was haunting Naila as she thought that their love would get limited to emails, and meeting up would get limited to phone calls. She was totally bugged with the idea that her passionate lover would soon become a normal email lover. It was certainly something new for Taruj as well. Waking up and not seeing Naila, not feeling the splash of her heated breath, not seeing her eyes that had a million expressions, were certainly not amusing ideas for him either.

"I miss you my Miss Glass."

He said on phone one fine night.

"I miss you too my Mr. Despo." Naila replied as she sighed heavily to his absence.

"Oh, your eyes would have changed a million

expressions when you just sighed."

Taruj said it in a deep regret. Naila smiled and said,

"We'll meet frequently, right?"

The girl wanted a reassurance that things would never change, that he would never change.

"Ofcourse we will."

He gently replied, paused for a while, and then continued,

"I miss holding your face close to mine and see you breathe heavier. I miss pulling you close and see you growing shy. The softness of your hands, the shyness in your eyes, your long hair playing around your...."

"Ting Tong!"

Suddenly, the door bell rang and it spoiled Naila's and Taruj's moment of an incomplete romance.

"I got to take the door baby. I'll call you later."

Taruj kept the phone and Naila took a deep sigh. She kept waiting for his call for the next two hours. Her wait ended with a message that read,

"It's my college friend from IIT. He'll be living with

me now. It'll take me a lot of time to get free. You please sleep, my princess."

Naila kept her phone away. She closed her eyes with hints of tears in them and slept silently. It was Sunday morning the next day. The morning took Naila by surprise as she woke up to an early morning knock on her room's door.

"Someone sent these flowers and chocolates for you."

An in-house maid of Naila's hostel said as she took the door. She grabbed the bouquet of red roses and chocolates with a huge smile. She kept them on the bed and took out the card from the bouquet. It read,

"I miss the smile that must be kissing your face right now, my queen. I miss your eyes Miss Glass. You're going to kill me someday."

Naila loved the very feeling of that partial romance. She was totally drowned in this new, yet beautiful feeling when suddenly her phone rang. She grabbed the phone in no time and it was him.

"How do you like the flowers maam?"

He said in a seductive voice from the other side of

the phone.

"They're lovely." Naila replied as she started to grow shy of his voice.

"I'm so sorry love. He suddenly shifted with his entire luggage. I knew my love got a little irritated." He laughed as he teased Naila and she said,

"How can you be so sure?"

"Oh man, it kills me not to see your detective face right now as you grow suspicious." He mourned only to make Naila smile. Naila and Taruj were the names of a strong relationship that certainly was not going to die. They started finding romance in separation. They started feeling passion in pain.

A week later........

"I feel like I'm in love with a man from a different time." Naila paused before she could speak further. After a moment of silence she said,

"You're my sunshine that I had each day. And now it feels like you're my lost sunshine."

She sighed deeply and Taruj kept listening to all that she had to say.

"It's like a romance from the ancient times. I sure

feel like a princess even now, but a princess that waits for her prince."

This was a new feeling for both the young lovers. Taruj sighed deeply and said,

"But now you don't have to get irked with my boy thing. If you know what I mean."

Naila sadly replied,

"But now, I miss your boy thing as well."

"Oh, so that is what you miss?"

He teased Naila and the girl grew shy and said,

"I miss everything."

"Two months baby, just two months. And I'll let you know that kissing is healthier than talking."

Taruj replied in both sadness and smile.

"Really? Now if I take that, you would come upto me and say- sex is better than kissing. Does that mean I should have sex with you?"

Both of them laughed, remembering the sarcastic beginning of their relationship.

"I never knew I could be in so much love with a

man, a desperate man." Naila said as she still continued to laugh. They chatted inseparably throughout the day and the night. However, passing time increased the workload on Taruj. Phone calls, text messages, emails and chats minimized. Naila patiently started waiting for two months to fly quickly, before she could race into his arms once again.

Two months later...

"Hey baby." Taruj said on phone one day.

"Hi." Naila replied as she already sensed some stress in his voice.

"I've something to tell you Naila."

His stammering voice made the girl anxious and she said,

"What is it?"

"Naila, there's a sudden official trip that I am finding very hard to postpone."

There was absolute silence at both the ends. He again spoke,

"They're thinking of promoting me soon after this tour."

Naila was still silent and Taruj tried to persuade her further. He said,

"You understand that baby? People work for two years to get this kind of a promotion. I'll be getting it in just two months."

His words were followed by a longer silence, so he further said,

"Is that not good for our future?" Taruj literally insisted Naila for some kind of a response. Finally, the girl broke her silence and said,

"Does that mean you are not coming to meet me?"

Naila was straight and flat in what she said.

Taruj hesitantly replied,

"Sorry love. This is very important."

But before he could have completed, Naila disconnected the phone. She left Taruj in shock and pain. He felt doomed and gloomy. He was hurt with Naila's response. He peeped outside his cabin's window to gulp in some fresh air.

"I should have been happy with the very thought of this promotion. But your absence makes me gloomy. It fades away my happiness, Naila."

He was thinking all of it to himself.

"After years of being in so much love, is this the closeness and trust we share?"

    A momentary thought that Naila would drift away from him with this incidence jolted his soul. He took no more time in deciding that he would ditch the promotion only to prove his endless love to his lady. How could he leave Naila in pain after all?

He whispered to himself in a sad voice,

"I miss you."

He took two hours to rehearse how to turn down the offer that everyone around knew he was so excited about. While he was busy in his own thoughts, a sudden knock on his cabin's door took him with a surprise.

"Sir, some flowers for you."

He was left in shock and surprise and he hurriedly collected the bouquet of artificial red roses (He disliked real flowers being plucked, which Naila only knew). He grabbed the card on the bouquet that read,

"Surprise my love!

So you think it's just you who can play weird pranks? Here's a cup of your tea. Taste it."

He dropped the card down for a moment, looked up and smilingly said,

"She's going to kill me someday."

After a long sigh, he began reading the card again, that said.

"Congratulations to my prince. I'm very happy for the promotion. Does that mean I'm not sad? Untrue!!

I'm happy. You've managed to secure our future.

I'm sad. You've ruined our date.

But in the end, this wait only increases my love for you. I miss you."

Naila's surprise and her expression of love left Taruj in some pain. He called her up and said,

"I love you Naila….. I….."

His voice choked for more words, and Naila said,

"So, men with balls and humor cry as well?"

Her joke was met with silence and she knew it did

not ease his guilt.

"It's okay! Don't, please don't."

She aped his way to calm him down that he used to usually follow to calm down Naila, when they were together. He was deeply moved with her innocent trials to put him at ease. Her discomfort to see him fall weak, her stammering as she saw him in pain- all this made Taruj fall in love with her all over again. She further said,

"It's not going to be about the number of days we shall be spending together. It's not going to be about the number of kisses and hugs we will share. It's always going to be about the memories we make. And believe me, I have enough of them- sufficient to wait for my lost sunshine forever. I love you."

These memories got Naila back to her senses once again. Tara was sitting next to her, holding her hand.

"I have lost the memories that were enough to last a lifetime. I feel empty and dismal, as I fail to find his clear existence in my past life. Get him back mother, I'll make fresh memories with the man I am again in love with."

THE LOST SUNSHINE

Tara wiped a tear that kissed her daughter's right cheek and said,

"We'll revive those forgotten memories, I promise."

"That shall not be enough, mother. I deny losing him, after falling in love with him again."

She looked at her mother who stood close to her, but helpless.

"Go and cook food before my father loses his patience."

Tara smiled to Naila and started leaving the room.

"Come back soon, I shall be waiting to know a higher notch of the intensity of his love."

Tara smiled at her daughter and left her with endless shadows and a few clear memories. She returned two hours later to find Naila asleep. She looked at her daughter with love, and said to herself,

"I wish you knew that he never………"

Before she could have completed, she was startled and she paused, realizing that Naila had just moved.

"Hey there my little one!"

She greeted Naila, who woke up in amusement and said,

"I want to know more of him mother, please."

After making Naila eat some food, Tara began telling her the story further.

"His love grew for you manifolds and he fell in love with your voice as well."

Soon the two sank in the deep ocean of Naila's past.

"I love your voice, love."

It was probably Naila's first introduction to an emotional Taruj. He was deeply touched and had fallen for Naila once again. They bonded strongly after that incident. Minutes became days, days became weeks and weeks, another two months.

Naila was busy studying something in the canteen of her college one morning.

"Hey love, you look so beautiful."

Her phone buzzed for a text message. She smiled while reading the text and replied,

THE LOST SUNSHINE

"I'm busy baby. I'll talk to you later."

Fifteen minutes passed......

"Naila, someone dropped these flowers for you with the guard."

One of Naila's college mates handed over a bouquet of red roses to Naila, and she said,

"Thank you." She gently grabbed the bouquet and smiled. It has been long that Taruj had kept himself occupied in his work. Naila had overloaded herself with studies to fill his absence. She was taken aback with a beautiful romantic surprise that she knew only he could have arranged. She stood up smiling to the bunch of red roses. She said to herself while she was still looking at the flowers,

"Someone seems to be missing me today."

She quickly grabbed the card and was surprised to see that it was blank. Naila's breath started growing heavier, and for a moment, she turned around and rushed to the canteen's door. She opened it and scanned every corner of the campus as far as she could see. Dejected, she simply got inside and took out her phone.

"For a moment, I felt that you were around. Thank

you for giving me such a precious memory today."

Before she could have hit the send button, she was startled by two arms that wrapped her from behind. She dropped her phone and the card in amazement, and turned her face. There he stood, close to her. Certainly, he had grown more handsome in the last four months. A tear rolled down Naila's eyes. He wiped it and said,

"Oh, your big eyes Miss Glass!"

He sighed deeply and kept smiling at Naila who was still in disbelief and shock. Soon, she realized it was all real and she hugged him tightly. He wrapped Naila in his arms, and the two sank in the romance of feeling each other for quite a few moments.

"I don't believe this. I just don't!"

Naila said, partly laughing and partly in shock.

Taruj knew his surprise was a big success.

"I love you baby."

He whispered in Naila's left ear, still holding her in his arms.

Naila took a half day and three days leave from the college. Taruj asked her to immediately pack her bag. The two slipped away to Goa for a few days for a love dipped vacation. They were both exceedingly happy and thrilled to be together after a long wait of four months. That warmth, happiness of re-union and the satisfaction of feeling each other, took over the young couple. Surprisingly, words decreased, and they both started enjoying the cozy and heated spells of incomplete passion, that they shared through their eyes. They landed in Goa that very evening.

"Be ready to explore a few days of hidden surprises, my queen."

Taruj whispered in Naila's ear and left the girl intoxicated with the splash of his warm breath. Naila enjoyed every bit of his closeness, as she was feeling his voice, his touch and the warm tease after one hundred and twenty long days of separation. The *'Blue Bird Resort'* was their secret hideaway in Goa, for the coming three days.

"Which surprise waits for me at the Blue Bird Resort, Mr. Despo?"

Naila asked Taruj, as the two slowly marched towards the main entrance of the resort. However, he was so engrossed in Naila's feel, that he ignored her question. Instead, he said,

"You've certainly grown hotter in the last four months." The tease in his eyes and the seduction in his voice made Naila shy. She looked down while she still walked by his side. After some moments of staying shy, she said,

"Now, don't turn the topic, okay?"

"How would you know how hard it is to curb the boy thing, my love."

His words were heavy and his intense feelings were hard to be overlooked. Naila felt the tease and she loved being in his love spell once again. A traditional welcome at the resort already dipped Naila in the feel of an exciting vacation upon arrival. The Blue Bird Resort was a famous romantic location for couples on honeymoon and families in the hunt of a leisure vacation, away from the noisy streets of Goa. It was a huge resort that was built on acres of land that concealed all of its guests and ensured utmost privacy to them.

This famous five star romantic resort was mainly famous for two things. The first were its blue-green lagoon rooms that gave an impression of the Juliette balconies. It was unlikely to believe the royalty that the romantic small lagoon rooms of this resort offered. The lagoon rooms were also the oldest rooms of that famous resort. The second most attractive feature of that resort was its two secluded tree houses that fun filled the families and guests with adventure. Other than a private beach that offered the guests a dining option at the sea side restaurant of that resort, the resort was also famous for the variety of indoor games it had for kids and adults in different sections.

Naila loved the large and clean swimming pool of that resort upon entrance itself. The pool had an infinity view of the nearby sea and the *Aguada fort*. The resort offered three more luxurious dining options to the guests other than the sea side restaurant. But before the girl could have started inspecting every corner of that amazing resort, Taruj gently blindfolded her and took her by surprise.

"Hey, what's this?"

He kept quiet and silently kept taking Naila to some place. In less than ten minutes, Naila realized that they have probably entered a room.

"Taruj, shall I open my eyes?"

Silence...

"Hello??"

Silence...

"Okay, I take this silence as a yes and here I open my eyes."

Naila was excited and thrilled. As soon as she opened her eyes, it was all dark. He was not to be seen anywhere around. She managed to get the lights without tumbling over anything. She pressed the button on and her life immediately moved two years and four months back. She was standing in the middle of a small room with a messy bed. The walls had many freshly stuck playboy posters. The shelves had some books and magazines. Many cheesy posters were scattered here and there. A bouquet on the side chair caught Naila's attention and she jumped to take it. She took out a card from the bouquet that read,

"Open the door and read the name plate before you read any further, my love."

Naila, immediately, rushed to get the door. The name plate said,

"My love nest- room number 413!"

Her heart started beating faster, as memories started pouring down in her mind and soul. She quickly got inside with wet eyes and started

THE LOST SUNSHINE

reading further. The card read,

"That's where you entered my life from, room number 413- the love nest."

Tears started welling down from Naila's eyes as she further read,

"Play the flat pitch of your sarcasm once again, my Miss Feminist. What would I have been, had I not had you, my love?"

She laughed and cried at the same time. He entered the room from the bathroom and hugged Naila tight.

"Oh my little devil, why are you crying?"

She pushed him away and said,

"What makes you hug me? It's so clear that you are desperate."

He laughed at her weird sarcasm, which was a reflection of the past times when she hated him. He pulled her close, very close, and said,

"Who wouldn't be desperate if the girlfriend would be so hot?"

He kissed Naila passionately for moments to come.

The two sank in a night of soulful passion and made love. It was 9 pm and a knock on the door took Naila by surprise. She looked around the complete area, scanned the bathroom, but he was nowhere. She took the door as fast as she could.

"This is for you maam."

A door boy handed Naila a gift box and left. As soon as the door boy left, she hurriedly closed the door. She impatiently opened the box that had a beautiful red dress and a letter. The letter said,

"I know your size even now."

Naila blushed and read further,

"Get dressed my love. I'm waiting for you at the sea side restaurant."

She smiled to the very thought of how special he made her feel throughout. She took a shower and got dolled up, to make her way to the sea side restaurant. Taruj received Naila at the sea side restaurant and took her to the wooden floor for a dance. The two were totally lost in each other. He gently placed a kiss on her neck to tease her even more. Minutes of passion were followed by a romantic candle lit dinner in the open air, romantic restaurant. The night followed up with a romantic splash of two souls getting closer and closer.

The next morning was the time for some ultimate 'Goan' fun. Taruj and Naila explored the Aguada fort and some nearby churches. The guy dared Naila for some adventure water sports by the evening. A totally tiring day rested with a peaceful sleep at night, after a soothing dinner by the sea side restaurant of the resort.

Naila woke up on the second day of her adventure in Goa and was pleasantly surprised to see a room decorated with flowers, and a small card by the side of her bed.

"Here comes my surprise number two." Naila spoke to herself as she hurried to read what the card said. She opened the card and read,

"Karaoke night has something special. Hold your breath until its late night, my love."

Naila smiled to herself. As she was wondering what the surprise could be, the door bell rang. She rushed to get the door. It was Taruj with a small box of chocolates in his right hand. Naila did not give him a chance to speak and pulled him inside.

"Oh, seems like the lady is totally amused."

Taruj made Naila shy and he gently hugged her.

"What's the surprise?"

Naila asked him. It was clear that she could not wait till late night, and that was the most fun part for Taruj. He said,

"Patience my dear, Patience!"

Naila kept bribing Taruj of wild and fancy things daylong to get hints of what the surprise was. He ensured that he spilled out nothing. The night arrived and Naila dressed up to look her best. She wore a black colored bodycon dress and teamed them up with red pumps.

"Oh, you look so sultry."

Taruj grabbed her from behind while she was combing her hair.

"You never grow tired of my looks, do you?"

Naila asked him as he gently placed a kiss on her neck. He simply smiled at Naila and blindfolded her again. She was excited and very alarmed to the very idea of yet another surprise. Taruj safely guided Naila to the karaoke room, where the girl expected her surprise to be. As they entered a room, he left Naila alone and hid himself behind a big wall. Naila opened her eyes realizing that he had left her alone again in a room.

"Hello!"

Naila said to herself as she opened her eyes. She was shocked to see an empty and dark room.

"Taruj, are you sure this is the karaoke room?"

Naila was confused seeing no one around. Suddenly, her eyes caught the spot light that dropped on a couple standing at the centre of a stage. Another spot light soon dropped on the door near the stage. One after another, the complete stage was filled with lights. Naila was stunned to see the complete set up. It was a depiction of the auditorium number one, from the IIT Delhi campus where Naila had spent three months of her summer internship.

She smiled to herself and said,

"What is he upto?"

Soon, a play began. The curtains dropped down and a banner read,

"This is how the story begins!"

Naila knew it was something she could have never

thought off. She didn't know what to expect as soon as the room started filling with guests. Finally, Taruj appeared from nowhere and took a seat next to Naila. He said,

"Gorgeous, here begins the fun."

The curtain raised and the next one hour gave Naila goosebumps, as she realized that it was the inaction of her college play, 'The Summer Sunshine'. The next sixty minutes cascaded Naila and Taruj down the memory lane of their first feeling of love. The dew and mist of time cleared, and Naila once again felt she was newly in love. She relived the intoxication that she used to feel when she had confused feelings about Taruj. After an hour of love soaked stage play, Taruj dedicated a song for Naila and took her upstage for a slow dance.

"So, how fresh do you feel my love?"

Naila was speechless to what she had seen in the last one hour. Taruj could cross all barriers of time and come up with fresh ideas to surprise Naila every day.

"Why?"

That is all that she asked him, silently, as the two

kept dancing. Naila somehow knew this was not all. After a memorable time of being together, they started walking down towards their room.

"Why would you do all this yet again?"

Taruj was silent as Naila continued walking while looking at him. She further said,

"Why would you constantly remind me of our past?"

"I'll let you know everything tomorrow, my love."

He gently smiled at Naila as he opened the door. They spent the entire night in each other's arms. Taruj knew the depictions had made a huge impact on Naila's heart. He knew that he was so far, so successful. The night passed slowly and it was their last day in Goa. Taruj woke up that morning and saw Naila sitting by the side of the window. She looked puzzled. He hugged her and wrapped her in his arms and said,

"You are happy, since you love surprises and you're sad, because this is the last day of our vacation."

Taruj knew Naila inside out.

"Right." Naila replied, in both sadness and smile. She hugged him tightly and said,

"Don't go. Let's stay together, forever."

He smiled at Naila and said,

"Very soon, we will. I promise."

Naila looked at him like an impatient child. He laughed and said,

"I promise, the end to this day will be an end to your entire worries baby, forever."

His assurance gave Naila the much needed warmth. She gently kissed him and said,

"I love you."

He smiled at her and took her out for breakfast. They explored the underwater world during the day time. It was followed with a romantic lunch date. Naila kept wondering throughout the day, what the last surprise could be. He took Naila to shopping, before they returned to the resort. Naila was still waiting for her last surprise, and soon, she saw Taruj falling asleep after a long tiring day. She waited for him to wake up, but in vain. Naila knew he made every moment of their trip special for her, but she knew it was all incomplete. She thought to herself,

"What about the answers that I needed?"

THE LOST SUNSHINE

A tear rolled down her eyes, as she saw the time passing at a brisk pace. She stood up and went straight to the bathroom, where she cried and consoled herself for the next forty minutes. After she thought she was strong enough to get over it without getting her answers, she stepped out of the bathroom to sleep. She was simply left in shock. As soon as she entered the room, she saw numerous small cards stuck on all the 4 walls of that room. There was a huge card lying on the bed. Naila was in tears and totally ashamed of doubting his love and intentions every now and then. As she moved close to the biggest card on the bed, she was shocked to see its front, that read,

"I know you will be tempted to open the biggest card first. Open it last, please. Begin with the small card kept under the lamp and explore the room."

Naila smiled to herself thinking,

"He knows me so well by now."

She took the card under the lamp as instructed. It read,

"Two years and four months ago, you changed my world upside down. I never knew such a girl could exist in the world who could force me to drop her back and not let me kiss her even once in return."

Naila smiled, as it was a trip to remembrance. It was a flash back of memories, that how she made a forceful entry in his life at her will. Naila finished reading the card and moved to the first wall that had many small posters stuck on it.

First poster on the first wall read,

"I knew that you enjoyed my looks and cheap talks from day one."

Naila deeply sighed and shook her head in disagreement. She moved to the next poster on the same wall that said,

"It hardly matters if you deny it now. I know I was too hot for you to resist." She laughed and moved to the third poster on the same wall. This was a slightly bigger poster and it read,

"This poster conceals my life, the only reason I breathe now and feel alive. Darling, please turn off the light on your right."

Naila turned off the light and she was taken aback to realize that the poster was glowing in darkness. It took her ten seconds to understand that it was her picture on the poster. A small scribbling read,

THE LOST SUNSHINE

"Just in case you are convinced that you are my life, please turn on the light and move to the next wall of posters."

Naila switched the light on. She took some moments to recollect herself. It was all very touching and unimaginable. She slowly moved to the next wall and read the poster number one that said,

"Your condition number one was never fulfilled even once. I used to lose my mind and my character the moment I used to see you everytime. Not a guy thing sweetheart, it was your impact. Believe me, you're pretty."

Naila could not stop smiling to those small pieces of posters on the four walls. She soon shifted to the second poster on the second wall. It read,

"My hypothetical girlfriend, I won you in real as well. But how did you never think of what happened to your bra tag collection after that day? Please find a gift box underneath the table on your right."

Naila was smiling as she found a gift box. She opened it and burst into a loud laughter, to see that he had kept them all safe until now.

"Cheapster."

She said it aloud, and still in fits of laughter, she moved to the first poster on the third wall. It read,

"Having known that your 'summer sunshine' was me, how could have I let it go? My first kiss with you is still fresh in my memories, love. Darling, it was your first touch after all."

Naila, by then, realized that for some reason Taruj had been somehow, very brilliantly, narrating a sequential series of events, that made their love story.

"I'm very happy, but still confused, Mr. Despo. Why and how?"

She said it out loud as she moved to the next poster on the same wall that read,

"Patience my dear, patience."

She burst into laughter and her smile refused to fade now. She moved to the last and a very small poster on the fourth wall. It read,

"Now, let's get the cat out of the box, love. Go and see the card on the bed."

Naila slowly moved to the bed where the huge card

THE LOST SUNSHINE

was lying. She opened the card and found a huge collection of her pictures. Most of those pictures were unique and new to Naila, as Taruj had clicked them secretly. There were six pictures in total and each had something scribbled underneath.

Picture Number one-

"I saw you talking to yourself in the campus that day, when I first came down to your college to convince you to be my girlfriend. I fell in love with you then and there. You seemed unreal to me. How could one girl have so many expressions?"

Naila smiled and grew shy.

Picture Number two-

"I clicked this picture when I bribed you that I would come to pick and drop you 'safely' each day. You took a few moments of smart thinking, and somehow, thought that you were a genius. I fell in love with you the second time in thirty minutes that same day."

Picture Number three-

"This comes after a very long gap. I clicked your sleeping face soon after the night we first made love. I knew then and there, that you were my girl."

Naila had tears in her eyes yet again.

Picture Number four-

"I absolutely loved you in multiple colors in this multicolored dress of yours. I went down to get chocolates for you. I saw you sitting on the window. Not many people have the confidence to pull off so many colors at once. You sure looked like a queen of that castle resort in Udaipur."

Naila fell in fresh love with Taruj again. She knew that he loved her, but she could never get a hint of the depth of his love.

Picture Number five-

"I clicked this at the Udaipur airport. You were trying to hide tears while talking to your mom. Your eyes looked beautiful to me even then."

Picture Number six-

"I came back moments later at the airport since my flight got delayed. Your mother had left. She had her flight to Bangalore before your flight to Delhi. I saw you sitting on the bench and crying alone. I clicked a tear in your eyes, but never had the courage to leave you alone once again. I simply stood there behind the wall to watch you till you left for your flight. I loved you so much Naila."

A deep satisfaction had captured Naila's heart by the time she finished with all the six pictures. She knew his love was there to last till endless times. She turned over the card to read more. It said,

"My darling Naila, I love you. I have many words to say it differently each day. I have many ways to make it feel fresh and new every morning. But still, it would all come up ending to three magical words............"

The scribbling ended there. Naila turned it over to read more. It said,

"The words are..........

I love sex."

Naila laughed out loud reading what he had written. She laughed as she wiped a tear off her pretty face. The card further read,

"I can't see you crying my love, I just joked. I love you, are the only three real words that make sense to me now. Far or away, meeting or not, busy or free, expressing or not, at the end of each night and with the dawn of each morning,

I will still love you.

Now pull me out please, I'm hiding under the bed."

Naila was in tears and shock, but she also smiled and laughed. She dropped down her hand to get him out. Finally, he came face to face with her. Naila did not dare to look straight into his eyes. She was going through multiple emotions.

He gently hugged her and calmed her down.

"So my dear, now is the time for your anxious questions."

Naila was quiet in his arms, as he said,

"Why?"

He gently placed his hand on her head and said,

"I wanted you to remember how fresh it was. What we had between us does not lay with many."

He paused for a while. Naila started looking in his eyes as he further said,

"With surprises or without, with distances or without, my love for you will never change."

He kissed Naila for some moments and then said,

THE LOST SUNSHINE

"And the next question- how did I manage to recreate this magic yet again?"

He sighed and said,

"The magic is in your eyes."

He winked at Naila and she had started to grow shy by then. He further said,

"When we parted ways, you told me that I am your lost sunshine."

He silenced for a while and looked straight in her eyes, held her hand and said,

"I was, am and will always be your summer sunshine. I will never be lost to time. I will never fade away with moments. I am here to stay with you, to stay in you."

He passionately pulled Naila in his arms and whispered,

"I will never be your lost sunshine. I am your present and will always be the same."

He gently pressed his lips against her cheeks and brushed them close to her lips. Naila's breath had grown heavier with the advent of a fresh splash of hidden romance in her life once again. He touched

Naila's lips with his and faintly said,

"I'm real and will always exist for real my love- away or close, but always your summer sunshine."

With this much said, he kissed her passionately. The two slipped in romance and made love like they made it, for the first time.

The next moment brought Naila back to her present reality. She opened her eyes, feeling the freshness of the same love in her life once again.

"I feel him inside my soul, mother."

Tara gently grabbed Naila's hand and said,

"I'm sure you do. After all, a part of his always belonged to your soul."

Naila was silent as if a storm has just passed her way.

"I don't believe he has left me forever. I feel his existence even now."

Tara silently kept listening to Naila, but she spoke no words.

"His promises were true, his love was true. I remember he said he would never leave me alone."

Naila was assertive and rebellious of what her mother had said in the beginning.

"I don't believe what you say is true. I will get him back, I know mother."

Naila started weeping in her mother's arms as she went through mixed feelings. She discovered the fresh joy of being deeply in love. She went through the pain that her forgotten love might not bring back the joy of togetherness, even if she somehow manages to remember and relive it all over again. It was 7 pm in the evening now, and Tara departed with the promise of bringing back the aura of love as a bed time tale after 10.

Naila starting counting hours, as present without him, started seeming unreal to her now. She waited impatiently for her mother to narrate the story further, as those stories were the only places where Naila's pain vanished away with his existence. She was surely in love with him again, without remembering all of him by herself.

CHAPTER SEVEN

WITH YOU…WITHOUT YOU, STILL IN LOVE WITH YOU

Naila had started getting visuals and voices from her past. She had been getting fresh memories of her ruined childhood revolving around a dominant and aggressive man. The 'Chapter Taruj' had started casting its spell in Naila's life all over again. At 11 pm, Tara entered Naila's room only to find her tense and rolling here and there on her bed. Tara rushed to attend her daughter immediately in concern.

"What is happening Naila? Are you fine? Are you seeing something? Is something bothering you, my baby?"

Tara held Naila and grabbed her in her arms.

"I see this man you say is my father. I see shadows of a violent childhood, mother. It's bothering me. Has he always been like this?"

THE LOST SUNSHINE

Tara had a spark in her eyes, as Naila disclosed seeing images and visuals from her childhood.

"Calm down Naila. Once you get your memory back, you would know we learnt to live with it years ago, my child. It will stop affecting you soon. I promise."

Naila could not curb her anxiety and she further said,

"I see him hitting you while you are running away with a small child in your hand."

Tara's eyes lost their focus for a moment, and finally, Naila screamed and said,

"So that means it was a lie when you told me that he had just hit you once, and never before or after that, mother?"

Tara's eyes drooped out as Naila insisted her to reveal the truth. Tara spoke with a trembling and shaking voice and said,

"The child you see in my arms is certainly not you, my dear."

Naila froze for a while and her curiosity rose to an extreme level, and she cribbed and said,

"Then?"

Tara closed her eyes and said,

"The glimpses you are getting are from the time when you were just two years old."

Tara knew it was not good to keep Naila anxious and over thinking. Which is why, she decided to hurry up with the truth and further said,

"The small child that I am carrying is your little two months old brother.

Naila's feet lost their ground for a moment. She was amazed to what her mother just said. After a while, Tara further said,

"He died while your father tried to hit my head with a glass bottle, that accidentally hit his head instead. He was Aadarsh, and your brother, who died at the age of just two months."

 Naila lost her words for few moments to come. She had fallen more in love with the lady she believed was her mother, and a little more in hatred with the man who her mother insisted was her father. She hugged her mother who suffered from the pain of losing her small child and the next moment she yelled,

"How could you stay with an animal like him? He tried to kill you and accidentally killed his own son? Why wasn't he sentenced? After all, he's a murderer."

Tara closed her eyes and tears welled down thick and fast. She sighed and said,

"I was not a working woman Naila. Aadarsh was not my only child. I loved you as much as I loved him. He was no special that he was a boy and you were no less that you were a girl- atleast for me. For me, both of you were equally precious. I left your father after Aadarsh died, but I could not find better means to take care of you. I needed money to raise you up when my parents refused to accept me and you. He had also gone mad and frustrated, after he accidentally killed his son- the only person he actually loved on Earth after his father. He stopped drinking after that incident. He used to hit me before that incident numerous times. But after that incident when I came back in his house, he had hit me only once, when you were six, not five, my dear."

It was hard and harsh for Naila to realize that her mother's life had much bitter memories and experiences than hers. Tara cried in Naila's arms. The poor lady further said,

"After your brother was gone, your father never considered you as a part of his life. He has been in the sorrow of his son's death and could never get out of the pain of accidentally killing his own son. He was not jailed, no one complained, nor did I. I had to raise you. With time, he stopped hitting me. And now he's too old. I cannot leave him now. I have seen worse time with him. The life that I now have is far better than the one I spent with him when you were very small Naila. Believe me my child; I survived when I lost Aadarsh, since I had to take care of you. But I will not be able to survive, if I lose you like I lost your brother years ago."

Naila hugged her mother and said,

"I promise you mother, I shall live and surpass every shock. Nothing will kill me, for I know, my breath is your life as well."

Naila finally calmed herself down for her mother's sake. However, the harshness that her mother had seen in her lifetime had left a strong pain in Naila's little heart by now. For the next one hour, Tara and Naila had their dinner. Once they finished eating, Tara said,

"Did you see something else too, Naila?"

THE LOST SUNSHINE

Silence...

"I mean something that I don't have an answer to."

She left Naila confused, and thus, she elaborated,

"Do you see anything from the visuals of what happened with you on the 11th of August, 2013?"

Tara's face had a pale and terrified look as she finally expected some news of what had happened to her daughter that evening.

"No."

Naila replied in a flat voice and started looking outside her window.

"But I'm sure I would soon."

Naila's confidence was worth a mention, as the young girl had started behaving differently yet again.

"So, don't you want to know the story any further?"

Tara asked amicably as she cuddled Naila. Naila said,

"Mother, I saw something else too."

Naila's flat glare made Tara uncomfortable. She did not look straight in Naila's eyes and said,

"What?"

Naila stayed silent for a while and then she said,

"Is this all true, whatever you have been telling me?"

Tara was struck with a cool breeze as she realized something was definitely different about Naila.

"Tell me what you have seen Naila."

Tara was anxious even though guilt had started raising its head in her eyes.

"I saw my first negative memory with you, mother."

Naila's silence was terrible for Tara. It made the lady even more uncomfortable around her daughter. In the lapse of any proper response from Tara, Naila continued,

"I see you stopping me from meeting him, mother."

Naila was looking straight in Tara's eyes as she spoke further,

"I see you holding me back and asking me to choose one."

She was silent for a while and then she continued,

"But why would you do such a thing? If you loved him like the way you said you did, if he loved me the way you believed he did, then why would you do it?"

Tara stood up and went close to the window. She peeped outside and said,

"It is not easy being a mother, Naila. The memory you recall is of 10th August, 2013, a day before things changed forever."

Tara's voice had a hint of guilt, anger and pleading. Her voice cracked and choked as she tried to speak further. After some moments of struggling with her emotions, she finally managed to speak and said,

"It was the toughest thing for me to raise you up without much interest and support from your father. Then this man, this new man, in your life- he never went down well in your father's spine. He was totally against him and your relationship. But I never knew things would change this dramatically, that I had to come upto you one day, and ask you to choose one."

Tara had started crying by then. She sat close to Naila and said,

"Forgive me for once Naila. I turned selfish. I still think had I been on your side and his, things would not have gone this bad. It was our fault that you both had to suffer."

She held Naila's hand and sobbed, until the girl kept her hand on her mother's head and said,

"Whom did I choose then?"

Naila had tears in her eyes as she expected some specific answer from Tara.

"You chose me Naila."

Naila's heart sank to the very thought that she had left Taruj a day before he gave up his life for Naila's happiness and safety. She was saddened and broken to hear what her mother replied. She took a deep sigh and said,

"Did he ever forgive me for that before he was gone?"

A tear rolled down Naila's eyes and Tara said,

"I'm sure he must have. He loved you beyond words Naila."

THE LOST SUNSHINE

Tara's answer was not acceptable to Naila and she said,

"What do you mean he must have? Why aren't you sure? Did he die or did I kill him by leaving him for you?"

Naila's eyes had many questions. Tara calmed her down and said,

"You left home at midnight of 10th August, 2013, with him to explain to him that the two of you could not stay together anymore. The second day, we recovered your hidden blood soaked body in a car. He was lying far from where we recovered you. He somehow had all his senses and was still breathing till then."

Naila's heart was aching to the painful recalling of her past and she yelled,

"No, stop it please. Please stop it."

Tara fetched a glass of water for the young and sobbing Naila. As she handed over the glass of water to Naila, she said,

"What is happening Naila, do you see something? Please tell me what is bothering you, my child?"

Naila still had her eyes closed and a painful

expression had covered her face.

"I see some people hitting me, mother. I don't see him around. I see myself alone in a jungle. I can't handle this anymore. I can't!"

Naila fainted very soon after she recalled her first memory from the date she had lost her love and her memory. She was soon rushed to the hospital. She came back to her senses after six hours of being unconscious.

"How do you feel now, Naila?"

Naila could hear the faint voice of a mid-aged man asking her how she was feeling as soon as she started getting back to her senses. She spoke nothing, but she simply dragged her face close to her mother who was sitting on her right side, tightly holding her hand.

"I'm fine, mother."

Her first words, after she came back to her senses choked her mother's throat and she said,

"I'm sorry for straining your mind so much. I just wanted to know if he had attacked you in anger that night."

Naila was alarmed with what her mother just said.

THE LOST SUNSHINE

The girl's heart sank in some deep pain and she said,

"Why did you think so?"

Tara sighed deeply and said,

"He had given up everything for you. Even then, you left him for me. I always doubted that he might have attacked you and later he must have felt guilty, and that's why he might have hit himself as well. And now, since you say you see some people attacking you and you don't see him around, I feel my doubt might have been true."

Naila's heart was sinking in pain as of late she had started fearing if he had attacked her- the man who loved her beyond words, ages and imagination. A tear kissed her eyes and she held her mother's hand tightly and said,

"You think it could be true? You think he could have attacked me?"

Tara was silent as she saw Naila getting impatient. This love story had kept her engaged for days now. She was certainly not in any condition to handle a brutal and violent side of his love that could salvage her flesh and soul. Tara calmed her down and said,

"I don't want to believe in any of it, my dear. I am sure; soon, you will be able to recall the complete truth."

Naila was still anxious and she said,

"You think he had the heart to kill me?"

Tara could not see her daughter in so much pain and she said,

"No!"

It eased the girl, but Tara was ashamed as she knew that she had implanted a seed of mistrust in Naila's mind, even when she herself did not completely believe in the same. But a part of her was convinced that vengeance can turn lovers into killers and she always cursed herself for letting Naila move alone with him that night.

Once things were calm again, the doctor (who was in the same room when Naila had gained consciousness) spoke,

"What more do you remember about your past?"

Naila was silent for few moments and then she said,

"I remember somethings, not all."

The doctor noted the confidence and clarity in her speech that wasn't shy like it used to be in the past few years that he had been treating Naila. He looked at Tara, smiled at her, and said,

"You might not have noticed the confidence in her voice and body language, but I have. She's also seeing clear bits of her past now. I am sure that soon your girl will recover her entire lost memory."

Tara was happy and soon the doctor left the room. Naila, who was earlier facing the other side of the room, turned her face to her mother. Tara gently kissed her forehead and said,

"I'm sorry my little one. I am still unsure if the possibility in my mind makes sense or have I unnecessarily burdened you with sadness. But like I said, being a mother and loving a child like a father and mother both, is not an easy thing."

Naila looked at her guilty mother and said,

"No, I understand. I want to know more about him and me. It is important for me to know if he had the heart to kill me for vengeance. I want to know if the martyr had turned a killer. Would you let me know the complete story, please?"

Naila paused for a while and saw her mother's

guilty face. She knew that the guilt was there, because the lady had just made Naila doubtful of her beautiful memories with him. She smiled at her mother and said,

"Like you, even I believe he couldn't have done such a thing. Soon, I shall confirm it. For now, I still want to know how much more he loved me."

Tara felt throughout, that something was changing continuously in Naila's behavior. Even the doctor pointed out the same. She was happy with her daughter's recovery, as now they (she and the doctor) believed that Naila's mind was stable enough to take shocks from the past as well. Smiling, the lady held her daughter's hand and began,

"After a loving and rather caring and romantic vacation at Goa, you had given up all your fears regarding him in life. You were exceedingly happy that day, when you called me up from the Delhi airport.

"Tara, Oh Tara!! I'm very happy you know." Naila told her mother over the phone from the Delhi airport on the 22nd of November, 2011.

Silence………

THE LOST SUNSHINE

"I know you are angry with me. I know you did not want me to go alone with him. But believe me please, we are totally in love, mom." Naila insisted as she wanted a response from her mother.

"Does being in love mean living together before marriage?"

Tara was hugely miffed with Naila, since she had gone ahead with the trip despite she disapproved of it.

"My happiness matters the most to you, right?" Naila said as she tried to calm down her angry mother.

"Yes it does, but..." Naila interrupted Tara in between and said,

"Then that's it. I couldn't see myself happier than this. I could have never lived around a man like dad, mom. Please believe me when I say this, we are really in love."

A minute of silence between the two was broken by Naila as she continued,

"He's gentle and unlike what dad is. I love him and I know he's here to stay and not to leave. Don't worry please. I shall always be safe as long as he's around me. I promise."

Naila somehow managed to convince her mother and get her on Naila's side.

The time Naila had spent with Taruj at Goa was certainly the best time of her life. Eventually, the vacation at Goa started becoming a memory and Taruj started becoming busier than before. It had been five months now that he had given up his job to be a part of some startup, soon after he was back from Goa. It demanded a lot of time and energy. It was yet another phase their relationship was going through. Weeks of his absence had started bothering Naila, and one day she finally broke down. She was terribly sad over the phone as she said,

"Listen, if this is over for you, then let me know please. I can't keep hanging around a dead relationship anymore. You have changed and I can see that."

"Why do you have to make it so tough for me always, Naila?"

He said from the other side of the phone. She was silent and he continued,

"Why do you need me to do something fancy all

the time to keep assuring you that I am still and will always be in love with you?"

His voice was cracking as he still continued,

"I have been working day in and day out. I have hardly been eating and sleeping, and finally work and life are making sense to me in this startup. But without your support, without your trust, I have started crumbling."

He was silent, and possibly, more hurt with Naila's silence. It irritated him somehow and he said,

"Okay fine, you won't speak up, right?"

He paused for a while and again said,

"Right?"

She still did not speak a word.

"I'll do one thing then. I will leave this startup in a month's time and take up a job at Delhi, if that will keep you assured of my feelings for you."

He was deeply hurt with Naila's ignorance. She still had nothing to say. He silently said,

"I'll talk to you later. I'm very tired, I need rest."

He kept the phone down. Hours of his stressful

sleep were met with weird dreams where he saw Naila moving away. He would give her a chase down the lane and she would keep on moving away and away. A phone call finally ended his bad dream and he realized that he had been sleeping for the last 9 hours continuously. He immediately took the phone and saw it was Naila's mother. His heart somehow sank to some creepy feeling and he immediately picked up the phone.

"Taruj, Naila has been admitted in the hospital early this morning. She suffered a nervous collapse."

His phone fell down from his hands. He covered his face with his hands and cried out loud. He blamed himself for her condition. And in no time, he rushed to Delhi to be at the side of his ailing love.

Two hours of flight and an hour of a cab ride left Taruj at a hospital. It had been five months that he had seen Naila, and this was certainly not the way he wanted the meeting to be. He was ashamed and guilty of leading Naila to such a horrible condition.

"Son, she's been taking your name since morning itself."

THE LOST SUNSHINE

Tara informed Taruj the moment he entered the hospital. He looked sleep deprived and tired even as he started going inside the ward where she lay. It seemed that he had not shaven and had not had a haircut for long. He was looking clumsy as he inched close to Naila. She looked weak and worked out as well. She was tired and restless. The moment she saw him, she broke down into tears. He immediately rushed to her and hugged her. Feeling his arms around her body was the most satisfying feeling for Naila. He took minutes to calm her down and reassure her that nothing between them had changed.

"I'm so sorry, my love. I'm so sorry."

He was ashamed every moment he saw Naila lying down on that hospital bed.

"I grew selfish and thought just about my career. How could have I done this to my most precious thing."

He broke down and it made Naila speak,

"No, I am sorry."

He looked up at her and was going to say something, but was stopped by Naila. She continued,

"I have been the insecure one in this relationship of ours. You had loved me and trusted me from the moment you saw me. I could never love you or trust you that ways."

She was speaking with soft words those were faintly audible to Taruj. He tilted close to her face so that it could have been easier for him to hear what she was saying. Tara kept watching the two from outside.

"I knew you love me and had not changed. I just wanted some time with you. I piled myself under lots and lots of studies. I had started keeping really unwell for the last few weeks. I could not sleep for the last five days. I called you up to sort things out. Once you started speaking, I don't remember when I exactly fainted and who got me to the hospital first. All the while I have been conscious, it was bothering me that you must have gone through pain thinking I was ignorant to your sufferings. I tried to speak last night, but soon, I fell down."

He was probably ashamed of himself this time. He knew now that Naila's absence was not her ignorance, but her ill health. His heart ached thinking that she collapsed while he was still on the phone, but he simply kept down the phone thinking she was under the spell of her huge ego.

THE LOST SUNSHINE

He held Naila's hand and said,

"This has happened between us for some reason, love. Get well soon and I promise this will never come up again."

Naila believed in every bit of what he said. The girl started recovering fast in his presence. He shifted to Delhi for some time and began working from home. He rented a flat for Naila, her mother and him. Naila would see him sitting on the computer for 20-25 non-stop hours. She then knew that the fears and possibilities in her mind were just a piece of her own imagination. In a week's time, she completely recovered. Tara's presence kept the passion in seal, but a week later she had to leave for Dehradun, since Naila's father could not have managed on his own anymore.

"Please take care of Naila for a few more days, son."

Tara requested Taruj as she was leaving for her home town.

"I will, aunty."

He assured Tara and she said,

"The only person who can take care of her after me

is you."

She departed with a smile leaving the two love birds all alone.

"So, how's my Miss Glass feeling now?"

Taruj wrapped Naila in his arms and kept holding her close for minutes to come.

"This is the most satisfying feeling I have ever come across in my entire life, Naila."

He spoke as he was still lost in Naila's essence.

"Your smell, your touch, your breath and your heartbeats- they make me feel alive. There is nothing more special to me than loving you. Life is so easy in your arms."

Time spell bound the two madly-in-love young hearts and they both enjoyed the ecstatic feeling of togetherness after months of confusion and separation. Another week passed, and Naila was fit enough to step into her normal life. It was also time for Taruj to head back to Mumbai. He had started becoming stressed out lately. Despite being around Naila, he used to keep lost. Naila noticed this and before he would have left, she asked him to take a night off from work.

"You are going to leave tomorrow morning anyway, Taruj. Please don't work tonight. Let's make these few hours of togetherness special. Please."

Naila insisted and Taruj had never denied a word to Naila. He gently agreed.

"You still love me?" Naila's question somehow irritated him. He sat close to her and said,

"Why do you ask me again and again? No matter what happens, I will never backout."

Naila remained silent for a few moments and then spoke,

"I never said you would backout, I was just asking you if you still loved me."

Taruj sighed deeply and turned his back and went close to the window. Naila got the pricking nerve that was bothering him for the last two days. She stood up from the bed and went close to him. She hugged him from behind and said,

"What is it?"

He was still not ready to speak up and said,

"I'm afraid. You aren't mature enough to

understand this. Moreover, I'm afraid of stressing you even a bit."

Naila turned him to face her and kissed him gently on his forehead. Then she said,

"Try, maybe you'll feel better. Atleast you will stop staying in some weird stress."

He knew she had noticed the change in his behavior since the last two days they were together, but still not very close. He agreed upon a lot of persuasion from Naila.

"Okay, I'm choosing to trust you with this thing. Above all, I want you to know one thing- that I love you and this truth will never change."

He made Naila sit on the bed and held her hand as he spoke,

"My family has come to know about you, but with a wrong impression. They are highly against you and this relationship."

Naila's heart sank and she clutched his hand tight. He read the anxiety on her face and said,

"No baby! Don't worry please. You are my life. I can give up anything and anyone but you. This is not about any breakup."

Naila took a deep sigh and said,

"Continue then."

"This story of not liking you is not really your fault. It is a mixture of my past and also my idea of quitting the job. I have been keeping very busy for the last five months. The news of your sudden collapse made me anxious and I left for Delhi suddenly." He paused for a while and then continued,

"I had no idea that my continuous absence would suddenly bother them this much. They called up my friends to find out if I was fine, and got to know that I have come to Delhi to meet my ailing girlfriend. They got the news that I have a girlfriend while they all continued believing for the last seven years that I was still going to get married to Trisha."

Naila's heart stopped beating for a while and in no time she said,

"Who is Trisha? And why would your family stay under the impression that you were going to marry her?"

Naila's face had gone deep red in anger and Taruj held her hand and said,

"Please trust me. I have no one else in my life than you. Let me finish, please."

Naila calmed down upon his persuasion and he further said,

"My sister and her husband are very rich. Trisha is the younger sister of my sister's husband. She is based in India, and is an IIM qualified event organizer with some reputed firm in Bangalore."

Naila's face was clearly burning in jealously. Taruj knew the sudden explanation of some totally absent girl from the scene coming out as such an important person in his family's life was bothering Naila. He further explained and said,

"My parents had died in car crash years ago. They had left behind a lot of property for us four kids. Trisha's parents and my father's brother had taken care of us. Then my sister was married to Trisha's brother when Trisha was fifteen and I was just sixteen years old. Trisha used to be my great friend back then. My sister and her husband are rich and famous doctors in the US, like you already know. My family holds a deep gratitude towards Trisha's family. When I qualified the JEE examination, my sister was too keen to get me wedded to Trisha. She believed Trisha was a

THE LOST SUNSHINE

perfect match for me. She believed that the families had seen and faced tough times together. She believed that the two families shared equal social status as well. And she also believed that I and Trisha were great companions, which we actually were, but when we were not even eighteen. I never took things seriously, since it was not my age to take things in a mature manner. All that I fancied at that point of time was that Trisha was beautiful."

His statement made Naila angry and she stood up in jealousy. Her face had gone red and she yelled,

"Why did you get along with me if she was so beautiful and perfect for you according to you and your family?"

Taruj smiled at her red, jealous face. He somehow had always loved Naila when she turned jealous. He grabbed her hand and pulled her back and hugged her closely.

"My love, no one is prettier to me than you are. This is the story of the past that was never of importance to me. Had it been anything serious, wouldn't have I informed you? Don't we all have multiple crushes when we are small? Do we end up marrying all our crushes?"

Naila could not relate to having multiple crushes, as before Taruj, she had never fallen in love with anyone else. However, all that she knew was that she always felt intoxicated in his strong arms. She lost her worries for a few moments and said,

"Why are you so hot?"

He laughed and kissed her, and after sometime, when Naila was calm and in a condition to hear what he wanted to discuss with patience, he began again and said,

"So, my sister wanted my opinion and all that I said was- she's pretty. This was all that I responded when I was not even in the first year of IIT. And then in the last so many years, no one made a serious mention of Trisha. I have no idea why all of them still believe that I was supposed to marry her. They were all serious about Trisha and my wedding. And I forgot about the same in the last long seven years as a joke. Then I met you in the third year of my college and fell in love with you. Now, they feel your presence is unwanted and sudden, while I feel Trisha's presence is sudden and unwanted in my life. I have grown up now and I have chosen you. But I was not even thinking that they could be serious about a joke I passed on years ago. None of them could believe that I have a girlfriend."

Naila was stunned and so was Taruj. He further said,

"They believed I had ditched Trisha. Wherein, I have not even been in active contact with her. Some forwarded jokes and normal hi-hello messages- that's all the contact that I had with her, and that too, before I had met you. They believe it was serious. I hardly considered her even as a regular friend of mine. Wherein, they believed that she was going to be my wife. And now, they are in a state of shock. And it's not just my family who is foolish; it's her family as well."

Taruj quieted for a while and Naila said,

"And what about her? Was she serious about this family confusion thing as well?"

Taruj sighed and said,

"How would I know this Naila? I have not even been in casual touch with her for months or years now."

He further sighed and said,

"How weird is this. Who is anyone else to take a decision in favor of my life's most important decision, without my mature and serious consent? Who are the families to mutually fix, that sooner someday, they would marry me off to some rich girl named Trisha? She is very dear to my sister and this is why she has fallen in hatred with you, without even meeting you."

He stood up in anguish and said,

"It has just come at the wrong time, you know. I know I could have explained them everything had they not come to know about you suddenly. They were already annoyed by the idea of the startup, and now they believe that I lie to them and devote my precious time to you. They have also come down to a random decision that you are affecting my career. They also believe that you might have been the reason that I turned down their idea of pursuing PHD from the U.S."

Suddenly, Naila remembered that Taruj was a PHD aspirant and enthusiast before meeting her. And upon meeting her, he decided that he would not be settling abroad.

She interrupted him for a while and said,

"Do you regret?"

He sat down immediately and said,

"Ofcourse not, it was my choice. Are you mad?"

She smiled at him and said,

"What happened next?"

He looked at her for a moment and then said,

"When they called me up, they did not inform me that they know that I am in Delhi and that I have a girlfriend. When they asked me, I did not unveil that I am with you, since I thought it was not the correct time."

He paused, took a deep sigh, and further said,

"They suddenly lashed out at me, and believed that it's you who is the reason behind this sudden friction between me and them. It was impossible for me to convince them on the phone that I never had anything with Trisha that could have been considered serious for getting two adults married. I also had a tough time convincing them that you have no role to play, whatsoever, in disturbing the pace and decisions related to my career."

"Did they believe you?" Naila asked him impatiently. He said,

"Partly they did, but things went out of control when they somehow learnt that I am taking care of you alone. It was something that made a huge dent on the impression of your family."

This thing didn't go down well with Naila and she said,

"What do you mean you were taking care of me alone? Tara has been here throughout, taking care of me and you as well. Don't you know that? Didn't you tell them?"

He calmed Naila down and said,

"You think I wouldn't have?"

Naila looked at him and said,

"No, you must have."

He continued then,

"It was impossible for me to make them understand why your mother left you alone with me, despite you had suffered a nervous breakdown. They became so skeptic about you and your whole family, that they asked me to back off immediately."

He sat down and kept his hands on his head and sighed. Naila knew he was under deep family pressure. She said,

THE LOST SUNSHINE

"I wouldn't say leave me, if that eases your stress."

She miffed him big time even before she could have completed her sentence, but she still managed to let him complete her words. She began again from where she had left and said,

"I wouldn't say leave me, if that eases your stress, since I know it wouldn't. I know you love me and cannot live without me anymore."

She somehow eased his pain with her words and continued,

"We still have no plans of getting married anytime soon. Do we?"

He nodded in a no and Naila continued,

"So, practically you have a lot of time to sort things out. I am sure you will be able to make them understand things better with time. Have patience my dear, patience."

She giggled as she aped his voice. He smiled in some kind of a relief and hugged Naila.

"Everything will be fine, my darling. I promise."

Her innocent ways to try and put him at ease and her cute jokes made Taruj forget all the troubles for a while. The two melted in love and started to share a great chemistry. Taruj flew back to Mumbai the next morning, but things changed a great deal in their relationship. He started finding time to keep Naila informed of what he was doing and where he was, just so that the girl doesn't feel totally disconnected with him ever again. He still managed to find a few hours every fourth alternate day to talk to her. Things started getting normal between the very much 'in-love' Taruj and Naila, yet again. After two months, Naila started working at some office in south Delhi.

It was the beginning of 2013, when Taruj started gaining a lot of stability in his work. He started making money and started feeling stable- both mentally and financially. It felt that merry times were residing somewhere near.

"Baby, I guess it is time that we should seriously think about getting married in a few months time."

Taruj said, while he was on phone with Naila one day. Naila smiled and said,

"Finally, the wait shall be over."

"Indeed, it's been frustrating, wanting to be around but holding back due to money and time." He replied and after a pause, he said,

"Why don't you either resign and look for a job in Mumbai, or just take a break until we get married and you shift to Mumbai?"

He offered Naila a suggestion that she initially resisted.

"Well, what's my job got to do with this?"

She certainly could not understand his point.

"Don't you plan to shift to Mumbai after we get married?"

Taruj eagerly asked Naila.

"Ofcourse I would. But quitting the job so soon? Does that make sense?"

He smiled at Naila's question and said,

"I'll be leaving for Bangalore and meeting my family next week. Probably, we shall be engaged by the end of this month or the beginning of the next month. I believe I am stable enough to get married to you in three months time from now."

He was silent and so was Naila. After a while he said,

"Either request for a transfer, or better, you make a job change. You have some kind of experience by now and I have numerous contacts. You shall be paid higher for a better designation than your current one for sure."

They both mutually agreed that making a job change would be a wise decision for Naila. She served the resignation letter at her company the very next day.

"Naila, you've decided to quit working?"

Tara asked Naila over the phone.

"Ofcourse not Tara, I am just making proper arrangements to switch over to a better opportunity. We plan to get married in three months time from now. By the end of this month, we will get engaged. Then, in the next two months, I shall be off to Mumbai where I will start working again."

Naila replied, and her reply left her mother a little furious.

"Getting married in three months time and getting engaged this month? Is it some kind of a joke that you have just cracked, my dear? Have you decided it all by yourself? I would need time to convince your father first. You should have given me some time, don't you think so?"

Tara's reply made Naila anxious and she said,

"Like his no is going to affect my decision. You need consent from that man? Oh, my father, I mean."

Tara knew Naila was going to be sarcastic with this. The young girl paused for a while and aggressively began again. She said,

"When has he been involved in anything that has been happening in my life?"

Her questions were though bitter, but all of them were true. She further continued and said,

"I went through numerous ups and downs throughout my life. I never saw him around in good times or bad. He's been least interested in my life. Why can't you just accept that you are my mother and my father both?"

Naila was certainly not amused with the idea of involving her father's opinion in between.

"But we need to keep him informed, don't we? After all, we live in his house."

Naila was silent as her mother continued,

"What do you expect me to tell Taruj's family then? That you have a father, or not?"

Tara's questions were bitter as well; and apparently, all of them made sense too.

"Tell me, Naila. I'll keep it like the way you want me to keep it. But for that, we'll have to let his family know everything about your relationship with your father. Would they digest it so easily?"

Naila paused for a while and she remembered how his family was already skeptic about Naila and her family. A few moments of silence, and then Naila said,

"Fine, I can ask him to come to Dun with his family only by next month. I'll also shift to Dun by then. Is that time long enough?"

Tara replied,

"I believe so."

They both disconnected the phone, but were in great tension.

Fifteen days later……

"I'll move to Dun in a week's time now. How was your meeting with your family? And why did you postpone it? I mean, you had to meet your family seven days ago, but you have just been back. I hope all is good, right?"

Naila was in a conversation with Taruj.

"Yes, but they had some work so they were not in Bangalore. That's why."

He was silent. Naila said,

"And, atleast tell me, what happened?"

Silence………

"Taruj, speak up what happened?"

He took a deep sigh and said,

"They still linger with their first impression of you and your family. They had found it hard to accept your presence at the stake of Trisha's happiness. It was a very hard time convincing them to come down and meet your family once, for my sake."

He quieted for a while and said,

"I could not let them know the complete truth about you and your dad."

Before he could have completed, Naila interrupted and said,

"That's okay. It's not needed either. Tara has already convinced him by now. Your family would not get a projection of any rift in my family."

Her answer gave Taruj a breather and he said,

"We'll come at your place on the 22nd of Feb, my love."

Naila remained silent for a while and then she said,

"What if things don't shape up like we expect them to? Are they coming with a feeling that they don't have to necessarily say a yes? Or have you informed them that meeting my family is just a formality, but the marriage is fixed?"

Her questions had a deeper concern. Taruj understood all her concerns and said,

"Naila, I might have asked them to just meet you all once, but I am not backing out in anyway. And they know it."

Before he could go on further, she said,

"And how do you know that they know it?"

"They are my family, that's how."

Taruj managed to convince Naila and the two

impatiently started waiting for the much awaited day to arrive. Naila shifted to her home town a week later.

"Why does he keep on staring at me, every time I pass his sight?"

Naila asked her mother while the two were having tea one fine February afternoon.

"It's ok. You ignore it and don't get into a rift with him for now. That's what he wants, a reaction from you. You keep calm."

Tara's reply only alarmed Naila and she said,

"Be precise mom, what's wrong?"

Seeing Naila's concern, Tara said,

"It was a tough time convincing him of this relationship. He says its inter-caste and he's not supportive of it."

Tara's reply made Naila a lot more stressed. She said,

"I hope he doesn't ruin things in front of them now."

Tara kept her hand on her daughter's head and

said,

"He won't."

There was a long silence in between Naila and Tara, and a few moments later, Tara said,

"Why don't you ask Taruj of hinting his family about your father's attitude?"

Naila went into a flash back with her mother's question and she thought to herself,

"How should I let you know that they're already thinking the other way around about us? I believe they need just one reason to say a 'no' and get Trisha in their family. This reason might just serve the purpose."

She gently tilted her head back and kept her hands on her eyes.

"Naila, ask Taruj to help you with this."

Her mother said again and poked her for a reply.

"I can't. It will not give a good impression." Naila said it in a go. The girl was indeed facing a lot of heat.

"Yes, maybe you are right. Don't worry, Taruj, you,

his family and me are supportive of this relationship already. Just one man's disagreement won't make such a big difference."

Tara left the room and Naila was in deep stress. She called up Taruj and informed him of the complete situation. He was too anxious to find out that things were not in smooth shape at Naila's end either. He said,

"But you said your mother has fixed it with him already."

He was in a rush and he further continued and said,

"Now what am I going to do if some unpleasant thing comes up in between from nowhere?"

Naila was not pleased with his answer and in anger she said,

"Then you walk out with your family and marry Trisha and never show up again."

She had hints of anger and tears as she still spoke,

"Is this a good thing in process? I doubt it, because I have not been stress-free or happy even once."

She was miffed and very frustrated. Before he could have explained, she disconnected the call.

Naila was feeling the heat of the moment and she left his phone unanswered for hours to come. She fell asleep within the next half an hour and gained consciousness only after five long hours. She immediately rushed to check her phone. It had fifteen missed calls and a few messages from him. She jumped to check the messages that read,

"How can you still do this to me Naila? Is it just you feeling the pressure and not me? Why do you have to test me again and again and ask me to leave? Why do you come up with things you don't even mean just to hurt and test me?"

"Did I say even once that leaving you is an option? I am not getting peace from my family and neither from you. This was not the time to make it tough for each other. I was looking around for your support Naila. I believe you have slept. Talk to you later."

Naila felt a little ashamed to have taken out all her frustration on him. She texted him that very moment,

"Slept?"

"No." He replied.

"Angry?"

THE LOST SUNSHINE

"Yes." He replied again.

"Still love me?"

He called her up immediately, and the moment they started talking, she said,

"I'm so sorry. Please forgive me."

He was silent and so was she. After some moments of awkward silence, she again said,

"I said I'm sorry. What else do you want me to say now?"

Silence again...

"Don't you want to talk to me now?"

She wept as she got no response. He took a deep sigh and said,

"No matter if things go wrong, I need you to start believing now that leaving you is not my option. I still love you and will always do."

They made up and started waiting for the day they had to make their families meet. Soon, it was the 22nd of February.

"Hello, Mrs. Joshi. How is Naila doing now?"

Suddenly, a voice took Naila and Tara by surprise. It was doctor Arora who had come to check on Naila, and by that time it was evening. Tara realized it had been a long time that she had been telling Naila of her past now.

"She's fine doctor."

Tara replied as the doctor started checking Naila.

"All seems to be fine. You can now take her back. Ensure that she eats proper food and takes a lot of rest." The doctor replied while instructing Tara to take special care of Naila's diet.

Naila got a discharge from the hospital. She kept looking outside the window while they were still in the car. After some silent minutes, the girl said,

"I have many memories of him by now. Most of them are of happy times when he loved me and adored me. I remember some of it on my own, mom."

Tara was exceedingly happy that Naila had started getting her memory back.

"What you believe about him attacking me that night might be true."

A deep pain had covered her face and she looked

at her mother who was looking down, probably in guilt. She continued,

"I don't remember most of it. I still see some people attacking me and I still don't see him anywhere close to me."

Naila had empty eyes as she still continued to speak. She further said,

"I am afraid that the complete truth might haunt me till death, mother."

Tears had started welling down from her eyes and she said,

"I want to know more about my story with him. Please tell me, did dad ruin things for us?"

Naila looked straight in her mother's eyes and she said,

"No, he did not. We all did."

Naila was surprised with her mother's answer and she said,

"I don't believe this."

Tara held Naila's hand and kept her head on her lap, and began,

"It was the 22nd of February 2013. We had made good arrangements. We lighted up the complete house and we hired private chauffeurs to pick them up from the airport as well. You continued being tense and so was I. I couldn't see your father interested in any of it at all. It was hurtful for me, but I managed all the arrangements with you."

Soon, Naila closed her eyes to relive probably the last chapter of her life with Taruj.

"Mom, I'm very scared."

Naila told her mother as she helped Naila getting dressed up in a silk sari.

"You look pretty, my little one."

Tara said as she looked at a rather stressed out Naila.

"Don't worry my dear. All is going to be good. They are good people."

Tara's assurance was not satisfactory for Naila, as she knew that they were not holding a good impression of her family. Deep inside, Naila had fears that things would drag her away from the love of her life. Soon it was evening and the family arrived. They were all well settled and satisfied people. Highly educated and learned people with a great sense of manners. Unlike what Naila feared, they greeted Naila's parents with love and huge respect.

"Am I dreaming?"

Naila spoke to herself.

"I hope the journey was not tiring."

Those were the first clear words Naila ever heard from her father's mouth. She had always seen him staring at others and murmuring something to himself in disgust.

"So that's how he sounds." Naila wondered all of it to herself.

"No, it was all perfect." Taruj's eldest sister and her husband replied. They were the highly learned and qualified doctor duo, from the U.S. While the sister Astha was a gynecologist, her husband Varun was a senior lung specialist.

"Oh, so they are the ones who believe that I stopped him from being a doctor, the PHD one though."

Naila was keeping all her thoughts to herself as she continued peeping outside the window of the room, from where the drawing room of her house could clearly be seen.

"But where's he?"

She was scanning every corner of the drawing room of her house, but he was nowhere to be seen. Finally, Naila's mother spoke,

"Where are the others?"

"Oh, they are on their way." Taruj's other sister Vibha replied. She was a leading consultant in an IT based firm at Bangalore, and her husband Sushant was a technical head in the same company.

"What does she mean by the others? Does it mean that the whole family is coming?"

Naila thought to herself after her mother's question. It increased Naila's stress a little more. Taruj had two elder sisters and one elder brother. His parents had died years ago in a car crash. Since then, his siblings had been keeping him like a child. He was the youngest of the lot, and they had invested in his complete education and were supporting his living till the date he had finally managed to secure himself financially. Soon, the wait ended. Two more cars entered the compound of Naila's house. His brother Prashant, who was also an IIT Alumni and an engineer at a leading firm at Bangalore, entered the house with his wife Sakshi, who was a professor at some famous university in Bangalore. They were accompanied with their father's elder brother Pramod, whom they all treated with huge respect. And at the end of all, he came in as well.

He looked quite different. Naila had always seen him in casuals. He was well dressed in a black Armani suit, and had his hair neatly done.

"He's so hot." Naila smiled, thinking to herself.

Taruj looked around the complete area. It seemed his eyes were in search of the woman of his dreams.

"So, what do you do?"

Naila's father finally began talking to Taruj. Naila was hugely nervous all the while her father was speaking. She expected him to come up with some shit or the other. But he kept failing her for the next one hour till he talked with all of them.

"Is this real? How are things going so smooth?"

Naila jumped merrily as she spoke to her mother, when the lady entered the room to finally take

Naila outside. Tara simply laughed and said,

"Come with me now."

Finally, the moment arrived and Taruj's wait ended with Naila's first sight that evening. She was dressed up in a printed pink silk sari. Her long hair had been styled to one side of her shoulder. She looked beautiful in her splendid Indian attire. Taruj could not stop staring at her, and finally she was seated next to him. They sure looked like a match made in heaven.

For the next two hours, the families continued talking. Naila and Taruj patiently waited for things to end up in a harmonious note. After four long hours of chatting and knowing each other, the families finally waved a goodbye. Naila and Taruj were exceedingly happy that things had shaped up well between the elders. He privately found a moment with Naila before departing. Pulling her close to him, he said,

"You have never looked so beautiful to me before. Get ready to be my wife, my love."

He kissed her and finally left with his family. They both were unusually happy that things had gone so smooth. A day passed, then the next, and the next, and the next.

Seven days later.......

"Taruj, mom has started feeling weird of your family's intentions and seriousness about this relationship. None of your family members have called up my parents even once ever since they have left. We had to confirm the date of engagement and marriage. I doubt, they have made up their mind to get you married to Trisha, and not me."

Naila was worried as she was talking to Taruj on phone.

"No, it can't be. They know I love you. I have been keeping very busy, love. Give me a day and I'll confirm it with them. They have probably been waiting for me to call up, but I couldn't. Don't worry."

He assured Naila and she kept down the phone in peace after his assurance.

"It's all fine mom, you just worry a lot these days. They had been waiting for Taruj to call up, but he suddenly went busy. Don't think too much."

Naila assured Tara who had started complaining a

lot about everything from the past few days.

"That is fine. But they should have still called up, atleast once, to say that it was a yes from their side."

She replied in irritation and it took Naila with surprise.

"Why are you being so melodramatic now? It is already a yes, why to complicate it further?"

Naila replied while she was fetching an apple from the refrigerator in the kitchen.

"You are still too young for all this Naila. Keep it to your elders now. This is not a formality or a complication. They came in and saw you. Did they ever say it is fixed?"

Tara's reply did not go down well in Naila's spine and it increased the girl's anger. She kept back the apple in disgust and said,

"It already is fixed. No matter what you elders come up with."

Naila marched out of the kitchen in a fury and saw her father hanging around by the side of the kitchen, while she walked straight to her room. Tara entered her room two hours later. Before the lady could have said anything, Naila said,

"So he's been pressing you to behave abnormally. Isn't it?"

Naila made her mother angry with a comment she just made. Tara looked at her daughter for a few moments and then said,

"You are habitual of drawing your conclusions all by yourself. You should be inspecting Taruj for the correct reasons, not us."

Naila was somewhat hurt with her mother's rude reply and she said,

"Why have you started behaving weirdly with me as of late, mom?"

"It is because I have been keeping stressed Naila. Can't you see it?"

Tara had hints of worry all over her face as she continued further and said,

"I went totally against your father for this relationship of yours. I went under his skin and that is why he agreed to accept things gracefully. If they come up with such nuisance now, he will make it very tough for me."

Naila could connect with her mother's pain. Tara still continued and said,

"They said they will call and confirm things in a day or two when they were leaving. Your father has been getting under my skin now. They have disappeared from the scene whatsoever. That is not being responsible. I feel the heat as I am worried about your future now."

Tara's concerns finally made a place in Naila's head. She was angry and she called up Taruj soon after her tired mother left the room. Naila was very annoyed and the moment he picked up the phone, she yelled,

"What is your family upto now?"

Naila was blunt, as she had recently felt the stress that her mother had been going through. Taruj was somewhat taken aback with the way Naila was reacting to the situation. He tried to calm her down and amicably said,

"What's wrong baby?"

Naila narrated the entire story to him. He patiently listened to every bit of what Naila had to say, and when she was done, he said,

"Believe me, it's been a delay from my end. Don't get my family wrong, please. Give me some more time and I will fix it all by tonight. I promise."

He again kept the phone with a reassurance from his side. Naila started waiting impatiently for the night to come, as she was facing a lot of heat from her mother's end. She kept waiting for Taruj's call until 2 am that day. Finally, he managed to call Naila at 2.15 am.

"Hello." Naila eagerly said as soon as she picked up his call. He was silent, and his silence was bothering Naila.

"What's wrong now?" She assertively asked Taruj to speak up.

"Naila..." He was falling short of words and it made Naila's heart sink in fear.

"Speak up for god's sake!" Naila yelled at Taruj and he finally managed to get some words out of his mouth.

"They are talking nonsense."

That was all that he could say.

"Who?"

Naila asked aggressively.

"My family." He said.

Naila went into a shell as he began speaking further.

"They are coming up with the weirdest reasons in the planet and are asking me to still back out."

Naila's heart began to sink in a deep pain and she failed to handle the situation completely.

"You and your family are troubled people, I suppose. Why don't you all just go to hell?"

Naila yelled at Taruj in a fierce voice and it left him with more trouble. He freaked out completely and could not handle the situation with his usual ease. He yelled as well, and said,

"Why the hell can't you ever be supportive of me? If this is how I have to come up each day and beg you to believe me, then this is not worth it."

Naila had never seen him behaving this way. It was a certain shock for the young girl. She failed to judge what he was going through and made it tougher for him. In anger, he continued and said,

"If this is how you have to treat me at the end of

each trouble, then there is no point in being together."

Naila disconnected the phone as he was still speaking and wept. He did not call her back. He did not send her a message either. This was the first time he had said of parting ways, and Naila had her own conclusions for that. Finally, she got a hold of herself after hours of crying. She typed a text, sent it to Taruj and blocked his number. The text read,

"It amazes me how you came up with this brilliant plan of breaking up for the sake of your family's happiness, and probably, yours too. Sheer brilliance, that you just managed to put the blame on me, that it's me who has forced you to break up. I cannot be with you either- a man with no stand and no words. Goodbye Mr. Taruj Singh, this is the end to all the mess you have created in my life."

Naila did not wake up that morning. It was 10 am and finally, her mother came in. She sat close to Naila as she realized that the young girl was awake. She placed her hand gently on Naila's head and said,

"He called up."

As soon as Tara started speaking, Naila turned her face away.

"What has gone wrong between the two of you now?"

Tara gently pulled Naila up and spoke to her while wiping tears off her red face. Naila was still silent.

"I told you, you are too young to understand all the complications involved. Didn't I?"

Tara asked Naila as she hugged her daughter. Naila broke down in her mother's arms and cried.

"He wanted to know if you were fine and said that you probably have blocked his number. He wants to talk to you."

Tara had a flat pitch as she was informing Naila of what Taruj had asked her to convey.

"Will you now tell me the whole thing?"

Tara asked Naila and the girl began,

"First, you tell me something please. And before you randomly answer it in anger without meaning it, let me tell you that I am putting in a lot of trust in you and then asking you this question."

THE LOST SUNSHINE

Naila had a lot of faith in her mother, which the lady understood. She amicably said,

"Ask me anything. I will only say what I feel is true."

Naila was satisfied with her mother's reply and she said,

"Are you unsure of Taruj's feelings for me now? Are you unsure of his commitment for this relationship now?"

While Naila questioned her mother of Taruj's intentions, she had a lot of fear in her eyes. Tara could clearly read the anxiety in her daughter's eyes and face and she said,

"No. He still loves you. You should talk to him once."

Tara's reassurance gave Naila some air and she said,

"His family did not like something about us."

"And what is that something?"

Tara asked Naila as she started getting angry.

"I don't know. Before he could have told me what happened, I blocked his number."

Naila's answer irritated her mother and the lady said,

"This is not a joke Naila. Talk to him and let me know the complete matter."

Naila borrowed her mother's phone, as her ego still did not allow her to unblock him so easily. She called him up. He picked up the call and said,

"Hello aunty, is she fine?"

A rather concerned voice greeted Naila from the other side of the phone.

"I am fine."

She replied with a choking voice. He was silent for a while. After a deep sigh, he said,

"I love you Naila. You mean the world to me. Please start trusting me before it kills me."

His voice choked and he broke down. In tears and a lot of stress, he said,

"How can you do this to me again and again? Why do I have to prove it to you again and again? This is not just a stressful time for you alone. I have been facing a triple blow. From my family's side, from yours and your mother's too."

Naila was taken aback with the pathetic condition he was in, and she said,

"My mother? What do you mean by that?"

"Yes, I have been facing a lot of pressure from her side as well." He said.

"Tell me everything, please." Naila asserted and promised she would not draw conclusions before he completes.

"I called up my family and asked them to talk to your parents and fix the date of our engagement and marriage. They started behaving like they were shocked to hear what I said."

He paused for a while, sighed and further said,

"You were right the other day, when you said how I could be sure that it's obvious to them that despite it's a yes from them or a no, I will be marrying you only."

He paused for a while again. It was a long pause this time. Naila remained silent all the while and after sometime he began again and said,

"I know they are coming up with weird and nonsensical reasons only because they still believe that Trisha is a better match. They said 'what do you mean by marriage and engagement? When did we say that we are ready for that girl and her family?'"

His voice was shaking as he further said,

"I was taken aback with their answer and it made me very angry. I yelled at them in the middle of that conference call and said, 'what the hell is wrong with you all? How can you people behave so casual and ignorant about it?' I said, 'don't you all know I am marrying her, and for that, I need a date?'"

He paused and said,

"You are listening, right?

"Yes." Naila replied. He sighed and further said,

"Then it was a long tiresome session of convincing them all over again. I wanted to know what their problem was. They did not make anything clear to me though. They said that they would come up to Mumbai in a week's time and talk to me about it. However, I am certain that they want me to give myself sometime and think about you once again."

He was silent for a while and then, he further said,

"That's all." Naila was silent. It was a long awkward silence and finally, she spoke and said,

THE LOST SUNSHINE

"So what now? Are you going to leave me?"

He was certainly in pressure but not amused with Naila's question. He said,

"For once and the last time, please understand- leaving you is not an option in my life."

His answer relieved Naila and he further said,

"I will try my best to convince them. If they still keep on talking shit, I'll have to leave them. I can give up anything and anyone but you."

His answer was a deep satisfaction for Naila as it lessened her fears. Suddenly, she remembered something and said,

"But you said my mother has been pressuring you as well, right?"

Taruj was unwilling to open up, but after a lot of persuasion from the girl, he began,

"When you disconnected the phone last night, I was not in a condition to judge anything. I fell asleep. I woke up at 9 and read your message. I called you up again and again, and soon I realized that you had probably blocked my number. It scared the shit out of me. I just wanted to know that you were fine. I called up your mother and then..."

He paused and could not speak up further. His long silence bothered Naila and she said,

"Please tell me what happened then."

He was unwilling but did not have a choice, so he further said,

"She was rude to me, extremely rude, unlike what she actually is. She asked me if I and my family were serious about the whole thing. I requested her to first check if you were fine. She was unwilling to listen to me. But after a lot of urging, she finally made way to your room. After checking that you were fine, she asked me to do something that I did not expect to come up suddenly."

He paused for a moment. With broken words he further said,

"She asked me to choose one, incase, my family is creating troubles."

Naila was shocked to hear the way her mother had treated Taruj and she said,

"What? She asked you to choose me or your family?"

THE LOST SUNSHINE

"Yes." He replied with cracking words.

"She has completely lost her mind, I tell you." Naila was in huge aggression and Taruj said,

"I somehow convinced her that things will be fine and I don't want you to get in a tiff with her now. Not many people are supportive of our relationship. She's probably the only support by now. She must have been under a lot of pressure from your father's side as well."

Soon they both hung up their phones, but Naila started behaving differently with her mother. She spoke less and spent more time alone. It started bothering Tara and she finally said,

"What is wrong with you now?"

Naila did not look at her mother and totally ignored her question.

"Naila, what is wrong?"

She asserted and finally Naila replied,

"You have known him for so long. How could you be so rude to him?"

Naila had hints of tears in her eyes as she still spoke,

"You and he are the two most special people in my life. How would I be feeling seeing you treat him like that?"

Before Naila could have completed, Tara stood up and marched outside saying,

"I expected him to be a bit mature. Never thought he would create a rift between you and me. This is not a matter of being rude with him. I have full right over you and I am afraid to compromise your happiness."

Naila knew that her mother was going through a stressful time. She also knew that Taruj was facing a lot of stress and pressure from both the families. She decided to wait until he would have met his family and worked things out.

"Things could go this wrong. I never thought Tara and I will stand on two opposite sides ever." Naila said to Taruj on phone one day.

"Neither did I expect that my family would behave this way."

Both the young lovers were in a state of shock seeing the elders manhandle their precious relationship. No one spoke much, but they both had deep faith that none of them would back out.

A week passed slowly and Taruj's family visited him to discuss the matter once and for all.

"Why have you all been behaving so casually about it?" Taruj asked his elder brother and his sister who was staying in Bangalore permanently now.

"What casualness do you find in our behavior? Did we ever say that we are going to get you married to this girl? Did you ever say that the meeting was just a formality and you had already decided to marry her? You are still not big enough to understand the technicalities involved. We still believe that the family and the girl don't match our status and qualifications." His brother replied. The reply certainly miffed Taruj and he said,

"Since when have you become so hypocrite and shallow, that things like status and shit started bothering you atleast? Why don't you speak up your heart and say that you still want me to marry Trisha and not Naila." He was miffed, and he further said after a small pause,

"I might not be big enough to learn the sudden hypocrite ideologies you have started understanding now, but I'm big enough to let you all know that I am going to marry her at any cost." He replied with a lot of assertion.

"If you have decided everything all by yourself, then what was the need to waste our time and drag us here?" His brother replied in anger as he rose from his seat.

Hours and hours of heated up arguments continued for long.

"We cannot approve of this relationship. It's final, we don't want you to marry that girl. That is all."

"Why are you all being so stiff? I cannot back down. I love her." Taruj pleaded throughout.

"The family is too much into showing off. They hired private chauffeurs and decorated the house as if it was an engagement ceremony. We are unsure of the intentions and expectations they hold from this marriage. Trisha and her family are known. Why can't you just give things a second thought for once, for our sake? Atleast think of your sister. She must be facing so much heat since you betrayed Trisha. You remember she is your sister's husband's real sister, or not?" Taruj was not pleased with the idea of betraying Trisha and he said,

"You all have created this mess and not me. I have never been in a relationship with that girl. Why don't you all confront her and ask her if I have used her in any ways ever. And you want me to ruin three lives for the sake of making things better for Astha (Taruj's eldest sister from the US) and not face the real thing? You think I will ever be able to forgive myself?"

Despite Taruj tried his best to persuade his family, he was left in vain.

"I still believe you should give yourself sometime, Taruj. It is going to be better if you concentrate on your career and give this thing some more time. Even if in the end you feel she is better than Trisha, we will reconsider things afresh."

They left and his hopes of getting the families into peace faded, but did not die.

He called up Naila and informed her of the complete situation.

"I think we should give them some more time." Naila suggested Taruj.

"But that might not go down well with your family." Taruj was concerned as he spoke to Naila of the ramifications that her option could have had. He better planned of forcing his family for their relationship, as he knew in the end they loved him above all. He knew they would bow down to his adamancy. But Naila wanted things to become peaceful between the families. She also wanted Taruj's family to accept her with love and not hatred. She did not want to be tagged as a burden to the new family. She had carried bitter memories from her childhood and was not willing to be called an unwanted burden any more by people in her life.

"It's okay, I have just my mother to handle, and you have many. Let's try once again and get them to like me as much as they like Trisha. " Naila replied as she tried to calm him down.

"Are you sure Naila? What you are planning and thinking of, is practically very tough and might need a lot of time and certain sacrifices as well." He insisted as he was still more concerned about Naila and her happiness. The girl had made up her mind that she would finally get his family to love her as well and she said,

"I think I am." She had some kind of confidence in her voice that was also accompanied by some kind of a dilemma.

"Then give me a month or two. I'll fix it and finally, we'll get the families to come to peace." He promised Naila and hung up the phone after she convinced him to wait for some more time. She wanted to give his family time to think about their decision, while the family started believing that Taruj was giving a second thought to his relationship with Naila.

Naila told her mother only half the truth. She knew that her mother would have reacted badly had she come to know that his family was creating problems and not accepting Naila for the sake of some other girl. Which is why, she decided to keep Trisha a secret from her mother. Half the truth confused Tara so badly that at the end of all, she started getting skeptic of Taruj's intentions as well.

"You should go back to Delhi and start your job Naila. I don't think he's serious anymore." Tara was annoyed while she was talking to Naila, and cleaning her closet.

"What are you saying mom? This was my idea and not his. I thought you understand us better than his family. Please give us some time. Please, I request you to not judge him through this incident."

Naila insisted but her mother kept turning down all that she had to say. Naila went through a rather stressful time, as she had to deal with two miffed people around her now- one was her father who had always been in anger ever since the girl's birth and the second, her mother, who as of late, had been behaving quite furiously with the poor girl. She still had no idea where things were going. Taruj used to keep busy in work and eventually, things started getting strange for Naila as well.

"I had been calling you for the last three days Taruj!!!" Naila was dicey of his feelings as she was speaking to him over the phone.

"I had work Naila." He replied and added,

"I said I am busy and I will call you once I am free."

His answer somehow saddened Naila and she said,

"I would have been busy too, had you not forced me to leave my job, and for what? You said we will be getting married by April and it's already May. If things are not settling well between you and your family, let me know. I will move out of your life immediately."

Naila's disgust and her anxiety were all understood.

"I have not been pushing things abnormally, Naila. Wasn't this your plan, my dear? Did I not warn you that things would need time and would also need sacrifices? And regarding your job, even I did not know it would take so much of time. Why don't you rejoin your job?"

His answer only made Naila more impatient and angry. In a fit of extreme anger, she said,

"This is nice, Naila quit your job. Yes sir, done! Naila, my family has lost it, now you rejoin your job and go to hell." She was hugely pissed with the way Taruj had been dealing with the situation.

"Do you hold any responsibility at all? Do you realize you have ruined my relationship with my mother and her relationship with her husband?"

Taruj was silent as she further said, "You never have a solution or a specific answer to any problem. I don't have any more patience left. Either get this thing going or let's just end this now."

"Ok fine, give me two days. I'll fix it up."

His answer miffed her even more. Sarcastically, she said,

"So you could have fixed it any time. You were just not serious about it."

"Why are you making this troublesome Naila? I

have been travelling to my family three times every month to change their mind. I have been succeeding in doing so and they have started considering things afresh by now. You think I have been sitting with hand on hand? Accelerating in my career was the only way they could have gone sure about you. Isn't this what you said you wanted? Am I mad that I have been exerting day in and day out?"

He paused for a while and said,

"I have been keeping so busy with work, family, you and your family. When was the last time anyone bothered about what I was going through?"

Differences in opinion and distances had started lingering in between Naila and Taruj more than anyone else by now. He finally got things fixed with his family and soon the two families met again. Neither of the family members liked each other, but things still went ahead peacefully. Naila and Taruj were engaged on the 12th of July, 2013. August 31st of the same year was the date of their wedding. Despite things were totally normal now, something had changed between them.

"Madame, we have reached home."

THE LOST SUNSHINE

The driver suddenly reminded Naila and Tara that the two were deeply lost in the past while they were being driven back to home from the hospital. Tara helped Naila to get down and placed her on the wheelchair. While she was taking the young girl to her room, Naila asked her mother in amusement and said,

"We were engaged and going to get married?"

"Yes dear." Tara replied.

"Then why were you asking me to leave him on the 10th of August, 2013?" Naila was hugely confused all the way her mother was taking her back to her room.

"It was our fault Naila. You both were suffering a lot." Tara had guilt in her eyes. She left Naila in the room and went outside to complete her kitchen work.

"We were engaged and were going to get married. What happened then?"

Naila kept thinking to herself all the while she was alone in her room. She scratched her past memories, but could only recollect the bits that her mother had narrated to her by now. Finally, the wait ended and her mother came to her rescue and

said,

"Don't strain yourself this much. Have food, and I'll let you know the rest."

They both ate very silently that night.

"Why were we not happy? This is what we wanted in the end, right?"

Naila asked her mother as she took her to the washroom. Her mother gently replied,

"It was a lot of stress and family friction that had started rubbing over you, not him."

Naila remained silent for a while. Finally, her mother placed her back on the bed, and Naila said,

"Please tell me, what happened then?"

Tara smiled and began,

"Taruj was exceedingly happy that finally, he was going to get married to you. He had been busy planning a birthday surprise for you that month. On the 22nd of July, one week before your birthday, he insisted me to come over alone and meet him. He was in town and did not inform you about it. I had started feeling differently of him by then. I wasn't much willing to join his plan, but I couldn't ignore his constant pleading. I went ahead and met him at the *'café Novice'*.

Soon, Tara and Naila drowned in the memories of Naila's past life.

"Hello Aunty."

Taruj greeted Tara with a lot of love and affection.

"Hello." Tara replied amicably. She behaved nice with him, but the earlier warmth had died at the hands of family friction.

"It's her birthday on the 29th of July and she loves surprises. I have a big surprise for her this time. She has also been keeping angry with me. This birthday will sort things between us before we are married."

Taruj was hugely excited as he narrated his plan to Tara. Though she was not fond of Taruj like before, but she appreciated his zeal to keep her daughter happy. After learning of his plan, she left for home and he secretly started staying at a hotel in Dehradun- Naila's hometown.

"Mom, this is going to be my last birthday with you before I'm married. Can we be friends again? Please mom."

Naila had tears in her eyes as she spoke to her

mother in the morning of 28th July, a day before her birthday.

"Oh, my baby, you and I have been inseparable since your birth. There are no differences between us now."

Tara assured Naila and the girl started counting hours. It was evening on the 28th of July and Naila was on a call with Taruj. She was humble with him, though unusually silent that evening. She began speaking and said,

"Why don't you come over and spend some time with me and Tara?"

"I would have loved to baby, but…"

Before Taruj could have completed, Naila snapped and completed the statement, and said,

"But you have a lot of work to do." She sarcastically laughed to herself and kept the phone down.

"I'm going to get married to the man I loved for years now. Why am I not happy? Why are these differences more evident than ever before? Why is all this not making sense to me anymore?" Naila was talking to herself. She was standing close to her room's window at around 10.48 pm, and suddenly her phone buzzed for a message that read,

"Have patience my dear, patience."

With that message, Naila sailed into a flash of memories from her past. She smiled like a fool to herself remembering all the good times she had spent with Taruj. Suddenly, something struck her mind and she called him up.

"Why did you say to have patience?"

She had a lot of hope when she talked to him, and he said,

"Patience will make things fine between you and me, I promise."

Naila was not happy with his answer as she expected it to be something else. She kept down the phone and silently wept. She thought of all the good times when he used to surprise her with different plans. It was all gone, the magic had gone away. Naila felt the pain and she fell asleep. She was awakened at 12 am on her birthday by her mother.

"Wish you a very 'Happy Birthday', my child."

Tara greeted Naila and hugged her. While Naila

hugged her mother back, she realized her mother had a black cloth in her right hand.

"What is this?" Naila asked with glittering eyes and a chirpy voice that had suddenly gained strength out of nowhere. Tara blindfolded Naila and said,

"Surprise!!"

She carefully guided Naila upstairs and left her alone.

"Mom?"

Silence……

"Hello!"

Silence……

Naila knew it was something thrilling and brilliant, that her mother had planned for her by then.

"I am opening my eyes now."

Naila was immensely pleased as she opened her eyes and found a lit up roof.

"Wow! Not bad Tara."

She was hugely happy and she slowly moved close to the table that was placed in the centre of the roof. It had a small tape recorder that said,

"Play me!"

"Okay!" Naila said to herself, and smilingly she pressed the button 'play'.

"Hey Miss Glass!"

Naila's breath was intoxicated with the first words that came from the recorder. It was his voice. It was the same old passion that had made Naila crazy and had dragged her into love. Her happiness intensified as she heard his voice in that recorder. She smiled and kept the recorder on the table, and sat on the chair closeby.

"Gosh, you look so beautiful." It was marked with a long pause and Naila stood up immediately. She ran around the complete roof and scanned every corner of her house from the roof top.

"Get back darling, the plan is too brilliant for you to figure out." Naila smiled at his smartness and said,

"Okay!"

She came back and then the recording went ahead.

"Now, when you have finally settled down, let me tell you the three most magical words that changed my life."

Naila's eyes widened as she remembered a piece from her past when he had said that the three most magical words were, 'I love sex!'. She laughed and looked around in nervousness to see if her mother was still standing somewhere near or not. Before she could have reacted, the recorder played a seductive laugh and the voice further said,

"You look gorgeous. Please find the box beneath the table."

The recording ended with that instruction and Naila was certainly very amused. She immediately pulled out a box that was lying under the table. She placed that huge box on her lap. It read,

"Down the Memory Lane...."

Naila's heart started beating faster. She slowly unwrapped the box and opened it. She was left smiling, and with tears, to see a Canvera album that read,

"Remembrance...."

Naila took out the Canvera album from the box and opened the first page. It was a picture of Naila from the bus stop in Delhi, three years ago. She smiled at it and started reading the scribbling at the bottom, that read,

"You were so irritated when we missed the bus to your hostel and you had to wait for thirty minutes. You couldn't stand my sight for even thirty seconds back then."

Naila laughed remembering her arrogance and turned to the next page. It was a beautiful picture of Naila from the auditorium of IIT Delhi. It read,

"This one comes from auditorium number one. I took it soon after 'The Summer Sunshine' became a smashing hit. You looked like a soldier in your golden garb. I still loved you then."

Naila turned the album to the third page and found a picture in which he was kneeling down and proposing to Naila. It read,

"Your mother made this moment so special. I had a copy too."

A compilation of dozens of such pictures filled Naila's heart with memories. She turned to the last page of the Canvera that had one last picture. It was a picture of Naila in a printed pink silk sari.

"I never found you this gorgeous ever again or ever

before. You looked someone different- maybe my wife. I love you so much, my queen."

Naila turned the last page of the canvera album and closed it. She took a deep sigh and said,

"What sense does all of this make now? The magic is gone."

She had tears in her eyes and suddenly, two arms took her from behind by surprise. She could hear a faint voice in her left ear, that said,

"I told you baby, the magic is in your eyes."

She immediately turned around and it was him. She looked in his eyes straight. He kept smiling at Naila and said,

"Miss Glass, nothing will ever change. I will keep on getting you back again and again. I love you."

His charm was too hard for Naila to avoid. She tried too hard to ignore his magnetic smile, but she failed and finally, she hugged him despite being angry. Moments of silence passed between them and finally Naila said,

"You started behaving rude."

"You started imagining I'm behaving rude. I was

just too busy solving the other important things, my love."

Taruj replied as he placed a kiss on Naila's forehead. He knew Naila was like a child. She was impatient, naive and impulsive. His love for Naila had made him extraordinarily patient, mature and calm. She rested in his arms for some time, and soon, her mother came upstairs.

"Mom you knew about this." Naila jumped out of Taruj's arms and held her mother close to her heart and hugged her.

"Yes I did." Her mother silently replied, while holding Naila tight in her arms.

"Oh thank you so much. This means a lot."

Naila kissed her mother's cheek and the three finally celebrated Naila's twenty-fourth birthday.

"So, what is the plan for tomorrow?" Naila asked Taruj as the two were sitting on the roof top till late that night. Tara had already gone down by then.

"I have invited my family and your friends. It is going to be a hard party, just the way you like." He said as he smiled at Naila. Suddenly, Naila remembered something and said,

"Hey, by the way, when you texted me 'have patience', were you already home by then?"

"I was sitting right outside your window." He laughed for a while, but then paused and said,

"It is the hardest thing to see you cry and not being able to take you in my arms, love. I grow tired of explaining that you are the most precious one in my life. You never grow tired of doubting it."

"I'm sorry." Naila replied as she moved close to him and placed a gentle kiss on his lips.

"That's not enough." He grinned and set Naila in a loud laughter.

Naila dolled up the next morning, and all of them, Naila, Taruj, Naila's mother and her father, left for Mussoorie.

"Oh my god, the party is in Mussoorie?"

Naila's excitement had no limit, as the very idea of the birthday destination thrilled her completely.

"Why didn't you tell me before?"

She screamed in happiness. Taruj smiled and said,

"So that the chain of surprises could continue." He pleased Naila the most with his reply. One and a half hour journey ended, and they all entered the *'Orchid Resort'*. It was a beautiful old palace turned into a royal resort. It offered a spectacular view of the Dehradun valley from its royal palace-like fencing. The resort was a beautiful property that also offered the feeling of being in the lap of royalty. It had a huge gate, regulated with a barrier, and only cars with valid permits from the resort were allowed in the premises. Unlike most of the five star hotels that welcome leisure travelers to explore their respective properties all round the clock, this resort had fixed timings for the leisure travelers who wanted to feel the beauty of this resort for security reasons. The Orchid Resort Hotel was a center of attraction for various high end guests and VIP's. Which is why, the security was always so tight.

Naila ran around the complete fencing of that royal fort like resort that had an in-house heated swimming pool in addition to the outside swimming pool that had numerous sun decks arranged around the complete place. The resort was picturesque that also made it a perfect wedding location. It had a beautiful open air banquet hall that offered the spectacular view of the Dehradun Valley from the front side of its fencing. The resort was also a home to scenic beauty, with various colorful gardens and lush green lawns that attracted tourists across the globe.

The resort offered two dining options to its guests. One was an open air restaurant that gave a breathtaking view of the scintillating valley of Dehradun. The other was a roof top restaurant that offered the spectacular view of the snow covered Himalayas, all round the year. The place was nothing short of postcard beauty and also attracted painters from all across the country and globe- who were always eager to encapsulate the beauty of that resort in their paintings. Naila was extremely happy to be getting a chance to view the hills of her childhood dream and staying in one of the best resorts that the place offered. She was very happy to be present in the Orchid resort and was awaiting her birthday bash that was going to be organized in the ball room of that resort, later the same evening.

"I love it." She yelled in happiness the moment she entered the resort.

"You made my day." She shyly told Taruj and continued, "Dessert after dinner!" He laughed at her innocent bribing in lieu of his wonderful surprise. Finally, Taruj made Naila's family meet his family who was staying at the same resort. Things were not in the best of harmony as none of the families enjoyed each other's presence or company. However, it had started making no difference to Taruj and Naila.

"I don't care if they all don't like each other anymore. All that I know is- you mean the world to me."

He grabbed Naila's hand as she watched the two families behave cold to each other.

"I don't care either." Naila said with sad eyes.

"If that's true, then why do you look so sad?"

He asserted as he kept holding her hand tight.

"I wanted something else. I expected something else." Naila replied with a sad face and low voice.

"It's okay love. All that we expect can't end up being true. I love you and that is the most satisfying feeling for me."

Taruj managed to cheer up Naila. They spent the day completely together. The families had lunch together, but none of them spoke. Taruj was living in some other planet that day. Naila's presence and her company were the only two things that mattered to him then. He cared in the least how happy the others were. All he knew was that, he was soon going to marry the woman of his dreams.

The evening was a gala time as Taruj threw a beautiful birthday party for Naila in the resort. The banquet and the ball room were booked for her birthday anniversary, and he was enquiring about its availability for their reception as well.

"You love the place, right?"

He confirmed it with Naila, and she said,

"I love this place a lot."

"Then how about planning a destination wedding at this same venue?"

Naila laughed at his question and said,

"So you want to ensure that the chain of surprises goes on and on?" They smiled at each other. Naila was enjoying her birthday party, when suddenly, she saw Taruj moving away with his family towards the façade that had rooms. She saw her parents following them, ensuring that they maintained some distance.

"I hope nothing goes wrong now." She prayed as she started following all of them.

"When did you decide that it is going to be a destination wedding?"

Taruj's sister asked him out loud. Naila soon joined her parents, who were standing outside the room where Taruj and his family were arguing about something. They silently kept standing outside and listened to the complete matter.

"You all have not been really into this. Have you? I decided it all by myself. I love the venue and so does Naila, what's more to it?"

Taruj's blunt reply was too much for his family, and his brother said,

"Then why have you called us here? Why do you drag us in between to insult us again and again?"

Taruj was certainly not amused with his family, and he said,

"Do you all decide beforehand, that you will create a rift in every auspicious occasion of my life from now? I am getting married to her in a month's time, so is it not obvious that I should be doing it the grand way? Just like you all always wanted?"

"Yes we all wanted it the grand way, but not with her, with Trisha and you know it. You are getting married to her at your own wish, not ours." They replied. That reply was clearly audible outside the room where Naila was silently listening to the conversation between Taruj and his family alongside her parents. She froze with the name of Trisha unveiled in front of her mother. She turned her face to explain it to her, but she realized that her mother had probably missed that part. She sighed in relief and silently kept grabbing the corner, and listened to the discussion further. Taruj totally ignored Trisha's part as it was not even relevant to him. He said bluntly all over again,

"Whatever the truth be, the fact is that she is going to be my wife now." Heated up arguments filled the room for some time and finally, Taruj said,

"I need to attend the party now. I request you all to enjoy as well. Don't create unnecessary scenes again and again."

Before he could have come out and seen Naila and her parents listening to the arguments, they all hid in a nearby corner. Naila followed Taruj back to the party and her parents went to their room.

"Hey, all well?"

THE LOST SUNSHINE

Naila asked Taruj, as she chased him from behind.

"Yes my love. All is fine. " He replied with a broad smile on his face.

"We heard whatever happened in the room between you and your family." She looked at him and continued,

"Mom and dad heard you and your family talking angrily about something related to the wedding in the party. They followed you people to the room. I saw you all moving towards the room, so I followed up and found mom and dad standing outside your room and listening to the heated exchange of words between you and your family. We heard everything. I was worried that Tara might get to know about Trisha and react absurdly, but luckily, she missed out on that part. I know now, that they still agreed to the marriage for your sake, and could still not accept my presence in place of her in their lives." Naila said with a sad expression on her face.

"But what matters is the fact that I am marrying you and I love only you, isn't it?" She did not reply, though she smiled at him. He assured Naila that everything would be fine. After an hour of being at the party together, a waiter approached Taruj and

said,

"Sir, there's some problem with your guests. We want you to take care of the noise please. We have other guests too." Taruj's and Naila's heart began to sink and both of them rushed to the main building where the rooms were.

"We did not invite you all to come over and take away our daughter. It was your son who was after our daughter. Naila asked him to leave many times. It's your brother who never gave up." Naila's mother and her father were saying this as the two entered the room.

"Your daughter and you have trapped him. He's too innocent to understand this entire plan." Before Taruj's family could have continued any further, he yelled from the door itself and said,

"What is wrong with you all? I have not invited you all to this vacation to spoil her birthday." He was very angry as he pointed out towards Naila who was crying standing at the corner of the same room.

It was all quite for some time, and he further said,

"Whether you people like it or not, we are getting married. That's all."

THE LOST SUNSHINE

While Taruj's family stayed silent to what he said, Naila's mother reacted and replied aggressively,

"How can I get my girl married in a family with such in-laws?" Naila's heart raced as she saw a very different side of her mother. Tara continued in anger and said,

"I don't trust such people with my daughter. She's my only child and I have raised her with great difficulty. I can't choose such a family for her."

Taruj and Naila were silent for a while and finally, Naila said,

"Mom, what are you saying? You know that I love him and I will marry him." Before the girl could have further persuaded her mother, the lady said,

"Naila, I have told you earlier as well, and now I am repeating it again- leave somethings to your elders. This marriage is not on the cards anymore."

Naila's heart stopped beating for a few moments and the girl started sweating in extreme stress and fear. Taruj suddenly held Tara's hand, and said,

"Aunty please, you know how much I adore her. You know this thing very well that if anyone after you can take care of her, it is me."

Taruj tried very hard to convince Naila's mother, but it was all in vain. They dragged Naila away forcefully, and left the place in no time. He sat behind in the room, with his hands on his head. Naila kept rebelling and crying all the way back to her house. She was literally thrown inside her room for being so rebellious. Her mother, her only best friend once, yelled at her and said,

"Don't prove it to me that your father is right about my upbringing being wrong."

She left Naila crying and hurt in the room all alone. For the next two hours, Naila could hear the rising voices of a fight between her mother and father. It was like a flash back of her ugly childhood where she used to encounter and discover her parents fighting all the time.

"I was never in favor of this inter-caste thing. I wanted her to get settled with some good Garhwali boy, but you and your daughter come up with nonsense always. Now do you feel satisfied after everyone in the society will mock us?"

Naila's father was yelling at her mother.

"None of us knew that the family would be like this. The boy is not bad, the family is. I have no idea who Trisha is and I am sure neither do Naila know a thing about this." She was trying to calm down her irritated and abusive husband constantly. Naila's heart sank as she realized that her mother had not missed out on Trisha's part and that now, it would be very difficult to persuade her for Taruj once again.

"What do you mean that the boy is nice? He's nonsense like all the others. I did not like him from the day one. This is why, I never wanted a daughter. This is why."

He endlessly kept blaming Tara for all the unfortunate things that had happened and were still happening in his life, according to him. After hours of screaming and yelling, it was all silent, very silent. Naila was alone in her room and crying. She had been waiting for a call from Taruj, but got none. She tried his number but it was switched off. It was late at night and none of them had eaten, except the irritated and least bothered, but most aggressive, father. Tara entered Naila's room with a dinner plate in her hand. Naila was just not ready to listen to her mother, but Tara forcefully convinced Naila to let her speak for once.

"I am still trying to convince your father Naila, despite his family told me that he left a girl Trisha for you. I am still considering him as a future option for you but under one condition."

Naila kept impatiently waiting for her mother to speak further and the lady said,

"If Taruj agrees to leave his family, I will get you married to him." Tara's condition was irritating for Naila and she said,

"First of all- I know who Trisha was, and secondly, Taruj never had a thing to do with her."

Her confession did hurt Tara and she said,

"Since when did you start keeping secrets from me as well? And if he had never got anything to do with her, why did you not inform me of the same?"

Naila was irritated; and thus, she said,

"The way you are behaving now should answer your question that why I did not inform you about the same earlier. Had I told you about Trisha before, I'm sure now that you would have screwed up things with your idiotic conditions like you screwed them now."

Tara was irked with Naila's reply, but she maintained her condition, and Naila finally yelled,

"Do you know how ridiculous you are sounding right now?"

She looked at her mother in extreme anger as a tear rolled down her eyes. She further gathered her choking voice and continued,

"What do you expect him to do then? He should give a divorce to his family? Talk logically mom. It's his family, not his wife. What will convince you that he keeps me above everything? He has already been saying he cares a damn who accepts me or not. What else do you want?"

Tara kept listening to the young girl silently. Finally, when Naila quieted, Tara said,

"You are too young for all this Naila. You are just twenty four and he's just twenty six. You both are too young for all this, you know."

Naila interrupted her mother and said,

"You all were mature, right? You are fifty three and they were all above thirty five. What did you all do? Fight like morons in the resort?"

Naila's tone irritated her mother and she said,

"What else should have I done? They came into the room and straightaway started threatening us of dire consequences. They started accusing us of conspiring and trapping their son. It was too much for your father and the rift enlarged. Those things cannot be mended now."

"So we should suffer since our elders behaved like kids?"

Naila was not ready to accept anything that her mother tried to explain.

"Did he call you up till now? Did he?"

Tara irritably poked Naila, when the girl turned down everything she said. Naila was silent and her mother continued,

"No, he did not call you up even once till now. It is because that's his family. Now or sometime later, but definitely, he will leave you for them. And that will be too hard for you to bear, my child. I cannot let you go through that pain, since I know you are not that strong, that you will digest it."

Tara had a deep concern in her voice as she still continued,

"I just need an assurance that he will leave his family if needed, but not you."

"And what do you want him to do to prove it to

you mom? Get real please. Families don't take divorces to end their relationships. He can just assure you which he already has done. What else do you want him to do?" Naila had a point too.

"I need him to give it to me in writing and stop being around his family completely."

Naila was just getting tired of her mother's logic. At the same time, she was getting skeptic about Taruj for not calling her even once. She did not sleep that entire night. Soon, it was the next morning that still had no signs of him. She finally called up at the resort to get a confirmation. They assured Naila that things were fine soon after her family had left, and that Taruj and his family left in the morning after breakfast. Naila felt very weird, and something was very wrong about the complete situation. She did not want to jump to any conclusion this time, before talking to Taruj. She decided to wait and finally, her wait ended at night. She got a call from him.

"Where have you been Taruj? I have been calling you since last night." Naila cried as she spoke to him. He stayed silent for a while, and then he said,

"I did not want to complicate things between us baby. I knew if I talked to you before sorting the issue, then things can become worse between the two of us for no reason. So, I enquired my family about the complete situation and what they told me was very alarming."

Naila was not very amused with his answer and she said,

"What alarmed you so much that you kept away from contacting me nightlong?" He took a deep sigh and began,

"After you and your family left, my family informed me about how your father behaved. Once the rift began, he started abusing not just your mother in front of my family, but he also abused my family and me as well." Before he could complete his sentence, Naila interrupted and said,

"My parents reacted after your family threatened them of dire consequences if we went ahead with the marriage."

Taruj replied and said,

"I know. They told me everything, from the beginning till the end."

He paused for a while and said,

"I am not taking any sides Naila. Both the families

were at fault. But the abusive language from your father was just unacceptable."

Naila created a tiff with him over the same issue. She yelled at him and said,

"And the threats from your family face to face? Was that acceptable? They were calling me and my mother trapsters, was that acceptable?"

"See, this is why I refrained from calling you until I could have resolved the matter. I said I am not taking any sides, and to hell with everyone. But you make it so tough Naila."

Naila was, by then, not much interested in what he had to say. She bluntly said,

"My mother is disapproving the relationship now, until you convince her that you will leave your family."

He was taken aback with the way Naila started talking.

"I already said I will marry you no matter anyone wants it or not. What else do you people want me to do?" He asked Naila in a state of certain shock.

"Give it in writing and don't meet your family again. This is what she wants." Naila replied bluntly.

"And is that fine with you?" Taruj asked Naila in a deep shock.

"No." Naila replied. After a pause she said,

"We should not be together, you know. My mother will never allow me to go ahead with this relationship anymore. And anyways, you feel your family was right." It was very hard for Taruj to convince Naila. All that she said in the end was,

"I am too tired of all this now. I need rest for some days, maybe a month or a few. Regarding the marriage, it's not in the cards anytime soon."

"I promise you, it is in the cards, and in destiny too." Replied Taruj as he kept the phone down. Naila wept for the next many hours. Days started passing by and there was his complete absence from her life. Naila's mother spent a lot of time with her for all those days she was depressed. One day, her mother suddenly said,

"I'm glad you chose me above him."

To which, Naila never responded. Naila became more and more silent with each passing day.

"Why do you still wear this engagement ring?"

Tara said, in the evening of 9th of august, 2013.

"Naila, I'm talking to you."

Tara gently took Naila's hand in between her hands and said,

"I just feel scared when I think of your future in that family, my child. And when you asked him to give up his family, he left you. Didn't he?"

"No, he never left me. I asked him to give me some time."

Naila replied as tears started rolling down from her eyes.

"Did giving some time mean leaving you alone completely? Wasn't he supposed to, atleast, stay in touch?"

Naila looked at her mother for a while and then replied in tears. She said,

"I know he loves me, mom."

The lady held Naila's hand and placed it close to her heart. She looked straight in her daughter's eyes and said,

"Then why has he not made a contact with you for

the last twelve days? Don't you feel strange about it?"

Tara asserted as she desperately wanted Naila to move on in her life.

"Rejoin your job in Delhi and move on, Naila."

"What move on, mom? I don't have the strength to be with anyone else after him. And you better get this thing down in your head now."

Naila yelled in anger, since her mother had been asking her to move on in life and for the last many days, she had been assuring Naila that she would find a good boy for her.

"Okay fine, I will not be forcing you for anything ever in life. Atleast, go back to your job."

With a lot of assertion and persuasion from her mother, Naila finally agreed to apply for a job in Delhi. She slept that night with her mother. The next morning came and Naila was hunting down some good jobs, when suddenly, one of Naila's old friends came down to meet her.

"Hello dear, where have you been for so long?" Tara greeted Poonam, Naila's very close and only permanent friend since her school days.

"Aunty, I have been keeping very busy. I have been teaching in a school and in the spare time, I go to the coaching for banking."

Soon, Tara left the two young girls alone.

"How are you Nailu?"

Poonam hugged Naila, and the girl started to weep.

"I have something to tell you." Poonam immediately stood up and closed the door, while she continued,

"Taruj has been in the city for the last seven days. He has been trying to call you, but he said that you have blocked his number. He has been calling aunty, but she has constantly been asking him to leave, since you have made up your mind to marry uncle's friend's son, right?"

Naila was shocked with the revelations that Poonam just made, and she said,

"What the hell are you talking about? I did not block his number. Had he called up mom, she would have definitely told me." Naila was certainly in a shock. Poonam disagreed with what Naila said, and she further began,

"He has been calling your mother dear. He called

up aunty five times in front of me. He has sent a letter for you."

Naila had tears in her eyes by then. Poonam took out the letter from her bag. The letter read,

"Hey Miss Glass,

These have been really bad mornings you know. Not seeing your face is so tough Naila. I miss you. Please forgive me if something has hurt you this much. Please give me one last chance. I know what has happened has hurt you, but let me change what's happened. I will meet you up at midnight, my Cinderella. I will come to take you with me and then, we shall not part again.

Taruj"

Naila had tears in her eyes by the time she finished reading the letter.

"How can mom do all this to me?"

Before the girls could have talked any further, Tara started banging on the door.

"Why have you two closed the door?"

Naila immediately hid the letter and Poonam got the door.

"Aunty we thought of trying some dresses, that's why."

Tara smiled at Poonam and said,

"Find out a little time these days and stay with Naila. She needs your company."

Tara left the room, and soon, Poonam departed with a letter that Naila had sent for Taruj. The whole afternoon, Naila stayed away from her mother. She was still in shock and disbelief for what her mother had been doing to her. She skipped her meals totally. In the evening, she went upstairs and sat on the roof of her house. She had carried her phone alongside. She checked her contact list when no one was around, and she found his number in the blocked list. Naila immediately unblocked his number and said to herself,

"I never knew she could do this to me."

Before she could have called up Taruj, Tara came upstairs.

"So he found a way to contact you at last."

Naila immediately turned around in shock and saw her mother standing close to the door with a letter in her right hand. Naila gave her a big stare and started looking away.

"Naila, I am not a villain. I'm your mother." Tara said as she came close to Naila. Naila was startled with what her mother said and she yelled and replied,

"No, you can't be my mother. Am I your real child? The way your husband treated me lifelong made me skeptic if he's my real father. What you did is way cheaper than what he had been doing to me since my childhood. Are you my real mother?"

Naila was deeply hurt with what her mother had done to her and Taruj. Before her mother could have spoken a word, she said,

"Where will you find a guy like him now? Who can keep up with my mood swings and still love me more with each passing day- some son of your husband's friend? Are you trying to get me married, or are you selling me to someone?"

Tara immediately slapped Naila and said,

"Enough, I'm your real mother and no, I am not selling you to anyone but trying to find a better family for you. The one who doesn't end up killing you or getting you killed."

Naila became quiet as she saw her mother break down. The terribly weak and old lady grabbed a corner of the rooftop and sat silently, while looking up at the evening sky. After moments of silence, she began,

"I have my fears regarding Taruj now. I tried convincing your father, but one thing that he says amongst many other wrong things is right. What if he ends up leaving you for his family after he gets married to you?"

Tara's eyes had gone wet and red by then. With trembling voice and shaking hands she continued,

"I met this boy Avinash about one year ago. Your father wanted me to marry you off to him. He is a nice boy. I turned down the proposal of your marriage since I knew about you and Taruj then. Of late, I have been wary of this boy Taruj. He loves you, but I don't know how much and until when that love will last against his family's will."

Tara took a deep sigh and said,

"Yes, I blocked his number from your phone and I did not allow him to meet you. That's not because I was planning to sell you off to some man. That was because I was trying to mend your life, Naila."

Naila realized she had ended up hurting her mother way too much. She sat down close to her mother and said,

"He has been in the city and begging you for the last one week. Could you not feel the pain he was going through even once?"

Naila had thick tears in her eyes as she further asked her mother and said,

"Could you not see how hurt I was with his absence and how difficult it was for me to even breathe in his complete absence?"

The young girl broke down and her mother finally said,

"I have been feeling your pain and his too. But I want both of you to understand now, that this marriage cannot happen. No matter if you marry Avinash or not, but I cannot let you off with a man I am unsure of."

Naila tried her heart out to convince her mother, but the old lady could not give up her fears at all. Finally, upon a lot of persuasion from Naila, she said,

"Now it's time for you to choose one. I gave up all

my happiness for you. I kept your happiness way ahead of mine. I brought you up like your mother and your father. Now, if you want to leave me behind for a man in your life, I will not stop you."

Tara left Naila alone and the poor girl kept weeping under the night sky for many hours to come.

CHAPTER EIGHT

A HOPE TO FIND MY? (LOVE AGAIN)

Naila's heart stopped beating for some moments to come. The very thought of leaving either one of her precious belongings broke her heart again and again. She was lost in pain and finally, she got a call from the man she loved.

"Hey, Miss Glass!"

Silence…

Naila lost all her worries for few seconds as she heard his voice. His presence in itself was a stress buster and the girl was lost in love for some time.

"I got your letter, my love." He paused for a few moments and then continued,

"I could finally breathe after twelve stressful days, after knowing that you were not marrying someone else."

His statement brought Naila back to reality and she

realized that they both were facing a very stressful and testing situation in their relationship. She had tears in her eyes and with a choking throat she said,

"I have to choose one, between you and my mother now." He was silent after Naila spoke. He took a deep sigh and said,

"I left everyone behind to be with you. I cannot imagine a life without my little Miss Feminist in it. "

Naila felt hopeless and indecisive, as both the persons concerned were her lifelines. She wept and replied,

"No matter who I choose, I love you both."

She sat down and cried endlessly. It was 10 pm when she finally went downstairs. She looked nowhere else, but moved straight to her room. She started packing her handbag. Tara came in that very moment while Naila was busy packing her essentials.

"So, it was this easy for you to leave me Naila?"

Naila did not respond and continued packing the handbag.

"I gave up my….." Before her mother could have

continued any further, she yelled in extreme fury and said,

"You gave up all your life and happiness to raise me like my mother and father both."

She looked straight in her mother's silent eyes. Tara could sense the painful aggression Naila was going through. The young girl further said with a choking throat,

"He has left his entire family behind. He has left his entire world for my sake. I can't suddenly ask him to leave forever and never come back so casually over a phone call. We have shared our lives for the last many years mom. Let me go and handle things the better way."

As soon as Naila finished, Tara took a sigh of relief and hugged Naila. While she was holding Naila tightly, she said,

"I knew it. You love me the most."

Naila hugged back her mother and wept.

"Don't cry Naila. I'm sure you will be able to make him understand."

Naila was quiet all the while she packed her bag, and her mother helped her.

"Take care of yourself and get back home soon. In the end, what matters to me is your happiness, my baby." Tara said as she placed a kiss on Naila's cheeks that had gone red.

It was soon midnight. Taruj entered Naila's house like a thief, but was shocked to see her mother standing alongside Naila. Naila was holding just a small handbag and no suitcase. His heart sank with the very thought that she might have left him for the sake of her mother's happiness. With curious and scared eyes, he wished Naila's mother. All that the lady replied, and that too, rather bluntly was,

"Drop her back safely."

In extreme confusion, Taruj replied,

"Yes aunty, I will."

Soon Naila hugged her mother and said,

"I love you mom."

"I know." Tara replied as she kissed her daughter. Soon Naila sat in a car that drove her away.

"And then, I saw your car going away and away. Finally, it vanished. I had a deep satisfaction that finally I would be able to rearrange your life my way- the better way, like I thought back then."

Naila opened up her eyes on her mother's lap and said,

"And then?"

As Naila asked her mother to narrate further, Tara's face got covered with horror that was refusing to die out so easily. Naila calmed her mother down and further said,

"That time has now gone, mother. You can now relax. It was the past. I want to know what happened after that. Please tell me."

With broken words, stammering tongue, trembling hands and hints of sweat, Tara further began and said,

"I was very anxious the same morning, when you had left with him during midnight. Your father had no idea about anything. It was bugging me bigtime, my dear. I talked to you at around 3 am that very morning when you had left, and you had promised me that everything would soon be sorted. You had also said that you would be returning home by the evening. I was thanking my stars that everything was fine by then."

Slowly, Tara started losing her words. In anxiety and stress, she said,

"I kept calling you and Taruj throughout the day, but your phone was unreachable. By the evening, I started losing all my patience. There were still no signs of either of you. I expected you to be back by then. I started cursing myself for letting you go all alone with him."

She paused for a while and hugged Naila very tightly. In a while, she recollected herself and said,

"It is the worst feeling I have ever gone through, Naila. That night passed in extreme fear. By the next morning, I was sure something had certainly gone wrong. You had never kept me waiting in my entire life. You always knew your long absence makes me nervous. I informed your father. He just made a huge scene but did nothing to help me find you. He maintained that I created that mess and that I should solve it myself.

I knew it was useless to waste anymore time begging your father. I was concerned about your safety. I straight away went to the police station and made contact with his family as well. They had huge contacts and very soon we traced your last location. I was numb to know you were in Delhi. You never informed me of the same. I disclosed my doubts to the police and said that he might have kidnapped and attacked you."

Naila was still clueless what her past was going to unveil. All she knew was that her mother felt then, and even now, that Taruj might have kidnapped and attacked her in anger. But before the girl could have asked any of her doubts, Tara further spoke,

"I know that I might have been wrong. But I was as helpless then as I am now. Only you or he knew the truth. And the truth is a mystery even now. With my statement to the police, his family fell in a deeper hatred with you and our family. They started believing that being with you was a curse for him. Despite none of us was willing to see each other's face, we were still working together and very closely for the first time to find you both. Later that night, we recovered his blood soaked body. My feet had lost its ground by then. They were deeply mourning and blood was scattered all around. I had no support and no one to give me a clue of where you were. He was still breathing and faintly saying something even then."

Tara could no more hold her nerves, and she stood up and went straight to the washroom. In the meantime, Naila kept looking outside her room's window. The questions in her eyes had hushed by then. Tara returned after splashing water on her face. She hugged Naila and wrapped her in her arms. With tears in her eyes, she then began again, and said,

"The ambulance was on its way and everyone around was trying to save him, when suddenly his sister said something."

Tara was silent for some time and then she said,

"His sister was saying that 'He's saying Naila is in the car'."

Tara had Goosebumps by then. She continued,

"I jumped to where his sister was kneeling down. We maintained silence for a while as he faintly spoke,

'In the jungle, I have hidden her in the car'."

Naila was looking straight in her mother's eyes. They were depicting the horror they had to go through two years ago.

"Some of the cops and I rushed to scan the nearby stretch of trees. We recovered a car hiding behind some bushes. It had blood. A lot of blood my dear. They opened the car and you were lying inside, in a pool of blood. You were unconscious, but covered."

Naila's mother had tears as she further spoke,

"His sister rushed to attend you and confirmed that you were alive. You both were rushed to the nearby hospital. For all the time he had his senses, he kept taking your name. And then we faced a silence for months. You came back to your senses six months after the incident and when you did, you had no memories left at all."

Tara's eyes had grown tired and her throat choked for any more words. She somehow still managed to speak, and further said,

"I cursed myself each day and each night. My ego and my fears parted you from your love. You both went through some horrible thing that night. He either saved your life at the stake of his own. Or he tried to kill you but later regretted the same. I will be ashamed throughout the rest of my life, my doubts may be vague, but I still believe that he had all the real reasons to attack you and then regret the same."

Naila silently distanced herself from her mother and dragged herself close to her room's window. She was silently watching the moon outside. In a while, she looked at her mother and said,

"Had he attacked me with a motto to kill me, why would have he unveiled to his sister that I was in the car?"

Naila was confused and her mother held her hand and said,

"Maybe, he must have regretted what he did to you later."

Naila wasn't convinced and she further said,

"And why would he have stabbed himself to death, had he then wanted to save me, mother?"

Her eyes were curious as the only remaining truth in her story now was the mystery of their sudden violent departure. And no one had an answer to it. Tara could sense how anxious Naila was by then. She had narrated the entire story to her daughter, but this piece of the truth was a mystery to her as well. Tara diverted the topic to ease Naila's pain and she said,

"All that I know for now is that we all made you both go through hell. And by the time we could have realized, things changed forever."

Naila now had nothing to say.

"Naila?"

Silence……

"Naila??"

Silence………

Tara reached for Naila and touched her.

"What happened?" Tara asserted as she realized Naila was lost somewhere.

"Was he very weak when you recovered his body?"

Her words had hints of pain and her eyes had hints of tears. Her mother replied,

"Yes, he was barely breathing. It was clear that he had somehow held to consciousness in order to confirm that you have been recovered safely."

Tara choked all the while she kept answering Naila's questions.

"If that is so, how do I believe that he had the heart to hit me?"

Tara held Naila tightly and said,

"Maybe he did not have the heart himself, and that is why he hired some men to stab you to death, which he later regretted and in a rage to save you, he got hurt himself." Naila was certainly trying to dig very hard to know what the truth was. All that she could still see were some shady images from that violent past. She nodded her head in disagreement and said,

"I don't think so. He had promised me that he will never be like my father. He wanted me to know this thing ahead of anything else, mother. He could have never done this to me. I know."

Naila had tears in her eyes as she tried to convince herself that her hero had never turned a villain, that her love was still impeccable and pure. She sighed and further asked her mother,

"Was he somewhere close to me?"

"No, his body was lying close to the road and your body was in the car. But the car had his blood as well. None of us could know what the truth was."

Naila was silent and her mother spoke,

"Do you now remember anything that had happened that night with you both?"

"Not all. I see some people dragging me towards a jungle. He's still nowhere close in that memory of mine." The girl was worried and very anxious. She wanted a confirmation that he had not planned that ugly violent encounter that she had to face two years ago. A tear rolled down her eyes and she closed them for some time, and rested on her mother's lap. In a moment or two, she woke up panting and screamed,

"I heard his voice."

Tara was amused and she said,

"What do you hear, my dear?"

The girl was panting heavily and she said,

"I don't know if this voice is from the same jungle where I was attacked, but I believe it is from the same night when I was attacked. I heard a few clear words, mother."

Tara could finally see Naila in some ease. She held her hand and urged her to speak up, and the girl replied,

"'I love you, love. Everything is going to be fine. I promise.' These words are constantly ringing in my ears."

Tara's amusement melted down and she said,

"You and he had seen major ups and downs in your relationship. It might be something from those past memories when he must have convinced you that his family and I will finally come to peace some day."

Naila resisted and said,

"Then why did I not enclose it in my diary?"

Tara gently patted her back and said,

"Is it necessary that you had written every single word in the diary, my dear?" Naila was quiet while her mother further said,

"I agree that the diary was a summary of your love plunge, but how does it guarantee that you had included every single word of your story in the diary?"

Naila understood what her mother meant and the girl started looking out of the window silently again. She was quiet and it was clear that she was trying to recollect the bits of her past that rested just between her and the deceased Taruj. Tara grabbed her daughter in her arms and said,

"I'm sure; soon, you will remember everything, my dear."

The old lady kissed Naila and left the room. That whole night made Tara feel guilty to a great extent.

She could hardly sleep, and kept on wondering of the pain Naila went through in the past, and was going through in her present all over again. She had no idea what the future held for her child. It was soon morning, and Tara had not slept even for a single moment. With a tired mind, worn out body and aching soul, she began working her daily chores like any other usual day.

It was around 7 am that she decided to check Naila once. Tara used to be very careful while going into Naila's room, as the girl used to wake up at the slightest sound of her mother's bangles. Very carefully, she entered the room and fell down for a few moments. After a few minutes passed by, she gained her consciousness. Naila was nowhere in the room. Her wheelchair was not seen anywhere close to her bed either. The old woman rushed to check the bathroom and she was not in there as well.

Tara ran out screaming, and realized that the car and the driver were nowhere in the courtyard too. She rushed to grab her phone and buzzed Naila. Her phone was recovered from her room. Tara called up the driver, but his number was switched off. She started developing hints of weird possibilities by then. She immediately stood up and started rushing outside. Suddenly, the lamp on Naila's bedside caught Tara's attention. There was a piece of paper lying underneath the lamp. The poor lady immediately rushed to check the paper. It was a letter from Naila that read,

"Tara, I'm sorry I am giving you this trouble again. But the first person I needed to be with was always him."

Her mother's heart sank as she further read the letter that said,

"That night I did not choose you, I chose him. I said I love you when I moved away, but I never said that I love you the most. There was nothing like loving either one of you more than the other. I loved you both, and I knew that in the end, you would want my happiness. That's what you said as well. We left for Delhi that very night. We were going to get married in a court at Delhi the same afternoon. I still wonder what made you lie ever since I recovered the letter in your closet. Last night, it was no more a tiresome journey to scratch on a peel of my memories. I got all my senses back soon after you had left me alone in the room. But like I said, the first person I needed to be with was always him. You know where to find me."

Tara sat down upon reading Naila's letter, and soon she flew to Delhi and headed straight to the hospital where they both were admitted two years ago. With shaking legs, Tara passed the same wards and same corridors that she had last seen one and half years ago. Naila had been in a coma and was admitted in that hospital for six months, until she recovered and was flown back to Dehradun one and a half years back. She collected the painful memories when she first entered that hospital with Naila and Taruj bleeding that night. She soon ended up near the ICU ward on the third floor. Her driver greeted her there and said,

"Madame, she woke me up early in the morning and said you had asked her to inform me that she had to be dropped in Delhi in the same hospital where she was admitted two years ago. She had the tickets too. I tried to contact you, but you did not answer the phone at around 4 am."

With the driver's statement, Tara realized that her phone was on silent mode. The driver further said,

"She drove her wheelchair to the verandah and I collected her from there and accompanied her to Delhi. She is fine, don't worry."

Tara realized that the driver had no idea that it was

Naila's plan. She thanked him for being a loyal keeper and finally, she entered the ICU ward. There she was, sitting by the side of a bed, holding a hand very close to her heart. Tara gained all the strength she had and entered the quiet room.

"So, you finally knew where to find me again?"

Naila said as soon as her mother entered the hospital's ICU ward. It was all silent between the two as Tara came close to Naila. Naila was still holding a hand very tightly when Tara placed a diary on her lap. As soon as Naila saw the diary, she realized that it was the same diary that her mother had gifted her on her twentieth birthday, the same diary that had her story with Taruj, the same diary that her mother had said she destroyed soon after Naila had recovered from the coma. Naila looked at her mother in disgust and aggression, and said,

"You lied even about this?"

Tara was silent and Naila further said,

"When I asked you first to hand over the diary that concealed my story with him, you said you had thrown the diary away. Why did you lie to me mom? What good do you feel in doing it again and again? Do you like causing pain to me?"

Naila turned her back and started facing the other side, still holding a hand very close and tight. Tara was ashamed, but she kept her hand on Naila's shoulder and said,

"The doctor had warned me of not letting you know anything about your past. It could have killed you Naila. When you recovered the letter from my closet, I had no choice but to tell you the entire truth. Yes, I lied that I threw away the diary, since I could not afford to let you know the entire story at once. Had I told you that I had the diary, you would have never agreed to not read all of it at once. It could have strained your mind and I could have lost you."

Naila was still silent and the lady further said,

"I never had the heart to throw away anything related to you or him. I had always kept the diary safe with me, like the pictures and the memories as well."

As the lady was speaking, she saw that Naila was drowned in thoughts. To break that awkward spell, the lady further said,

"The doctors say that he's no more living. It's his family who…"

THE LOST SUNSHINE

Naila did not let her mother complete her statement and immediately looked up and said,

"Why did you lie about this thing to me? How could you have the heart to say so?"

Tara looked at her furious daughter and said,

"I did not know how to unveil this to you. We had no idea how you would react to this. It was the safest way to introduce him to you as your lost and gone memory. It was necessary so that you could forget it all in the end like a story and move on." Naila snapped that very moment and said,

"You could still be so selfish? Even after so much had happened to us?"

Naila had still been holding a hand very close to her heart as she further spoke,

"You tried to make me move on in life years ago as well, but he found me somehow." She immediately faced the man whose hand she was holding. It was none other than her love, Taruj. There he was, still lying on the bed, unconscious and unmoved, resting with his eyes closed. His silence was still speaking to Naila and she simply hugged him and said,

"We are inseparable. If he was there, how could have I died? If I am here, how could have he left?"

She silently cried as she kept her head close to his chest. Taruj was very weak and silent, but still breathing. Tara was ashamed, but she managed to speak and she said,

"We intervened in your story but could not set you both apart. Please tell me now, what had happened when you both were going to the court that evening?"

Naila looked up at her mother and said,

"By now, I am sure that you know that he had not attacked me."

Tara nodded in agreement and Naila said with a smile on her face, as she looked at Taruj, and said,

"See, I never trusted anyone else but my heart. I always knew you could never do all this to me."

Tara saw the strong bond between Naila and Taruj yet again. She was ashamed that she had lied about his death, but she knew she had done it all to ensure Naila's safety. And even Taruj would have done the same, had it been required of him. Naila took a deep sigh and began telling the story to her mother. She said,

"It was all fine by the time we left the airport. We had breakfast together and he hired a car for the complete day. When we left for the court, he realized, we were being followed. I panicked and wanted to call the police and inform you. But we realized that the bag was in the trunk. And both of our phones were in my handbag. Helplessly, he started changing the route. Soon, Naila drowned in the horrible memory of her past from the evening where they (Naila and Taruj) were attacked by some men.

"This Scorpio is following us Naila. Stay back and hold the seat tight. I promise I will save you, my love. I promise."

Taruj increased the speed of his car while trying to memorize the number of that white Scorpio that still chased them endlessly. Naila was too scared and Taruj knew this fact. He wanted to ask her to concentrate on memorizing the number of that car, but he could not do so. He realized the trauma that she was going through when he clearly saw her trembling legs and shaking body as she urged him to speed up. In between those strands of tension, he could not totally concentrate on speeding and soon the Scorpio with seven men took over their car. It seemed that those men were drunk and Naila had no time to react, and soon the men started attacking their car in that narrow silent road in the outskirts of Delhi. Taruj had ensured that he had closed all the windows, but it was all in vain. They soon damaged the car and pulled the two out. There was no one for help. They dragged Naila by her hair and threw her to one side of the road.

Naila's eyes were filled with horror as she saw them hitting Taruj mercilessly with stones, sticks and bats. She screamed for help while five men kept hitting him and the two others kept holding Naila away from him. She tried her best to reach for him, but she couldn't. He tried to fight them back, but it was impossible to win over five men with sticks and bats in real life. Naila was in shock, when finally Taruj lay unmoved and bleeding near the road. He was unconscious and probably dead. His blood had filled the grasses that marked the beginning of a jungle where those seven men started dragging Naila soon after Taruj had fallen unconscious.

She still did not know who they were. She had never seen them before. They started hitting Naila while they dragged her deeper into the jungle mercilessly. She thought he was gone. She was worried for him, she was worried for herself and for some moment, she wanted to die, and not live without him in this world, even for a moment. Just before they could have touched her, believing that Taruj was out, a car appeared from nowhere inside the jungle. He was driving that same car in which they were going to the court and were suddenly attacked. He was bleeding, while he purposely drove the car over one of those men. He fought them hard this time. They again used sticks and hit Naila's head and his as well. He was bleeding, but not giving up. Soon Naila fell down. She could hear some horns close by. It was then that those men started running away with the hint of people passing through that abandoned road.

Once those men disappeared, Taruj grabbed Naila's bleeding body in his arms and kept her head on his lap. Naila was conscious, but faintly breathing by then. Tears welled down from his eyes and he hugged her and said,

"I will save you, my life. I will fight till my last breath."

With this much said, he hid Naila's bleeding body inside the car they had hired. It was getting darker and he could barely drag his own weight. He still drove the car deeper into the jungle and hid it in between some bushes. He turned his face to see where Naila was and said,

"I love you, love. Everything is going to be fine. I promise."

She was silent, hurt and unmoved, but alive by then. He was unknown to the fact that she could listen to his voice and then, she faintly saw his shadow depart and he never returned for hours. Naila finally fell unconscious and woke up after staying in a coma for six long months.

The girl soon came back to her present, after narrating the trauma they both had to go through on the 11th of August, 2013. Tara cried to the sufferings they both had to go through for a few moments. She was also ashamed that she had doubted his pure love for Naila. She recollected herself and said,

"You were right that day. Where could I have found a man like him? Who could have loved you like him? I admit my darling, that he has beaten me in the chapter of selfless love."

All the while Naila kept close to him, her mother suddenly said,

"But how did you know that he was alive?" She had not even completed her sentence clearly and Naila said,

"When we were driven to the hospital in the ambulance, I had some senses and my memory as well. They were saying, his sister and her husband that he was unconscious, but alive. That's my last memory when I took a sigh of relief and knew deep inside, that he would soon be fine."

She kissed his hands and said,

"He loved me then and he loves me now."

"But the doctors say he's not going to make it to life again. Recently, the pressure on the ventilator has also been on an increase with each passing day. It's his family who just doesn't give up."

Naila looked up at her mother and smiled. She placed her head on his chest and heard his heart beating. She said,

"As long as his heart beats, he's alive."

With hints of tears and the incomplete intoxication of his presence, Naila hugged him and said,

"Wrap me in your arms the sooner you can."

She held his hand and silently wept for some hours. Soon, Naila's mother contacted Taruj's family and informed them that Naila had recovered completely, and gained her memory back. It seemed that the two years long wait of that family had finally come to an end. His brother and two sisters, all had shifted to Delhi soon after he was admitted in the hospital and had been taking care of him since then. Naila's recovery was like a boon to the family that had struggled in between the dark pits of imagining what had happened with their brother that night. Soon, they arrived in the ward and Naila informed them of the same.

The police was re-informed, and in the next few hours, Naila was interrogated thoroughly in a separate room in the hospital, since so many people could not be allowed inside the ICU ward. She informed the police about every minute detail that she remembered from that two years old incident. After a rigorous session of helping the police with every single detail, Naila headed her way back to the ICU ward of the hospital with her mother. The sun had gone down by then. The moment Naila entered the room in her wheelchair, she saw him lying on the bed, still unmoved and unconscious.

Tears fell down from her eyes as she had a deep satisfaction of finding her true love that she believed she had lost initially. She comforted herself around his arms, but ensured that she did not lay pressure on his body at all. He was not that strong anymore. Naila started living in the hope of reviving him back to life yet again. She also hoped that soon the culprits who had attacked them on the 11th of August, 2013, would be identified and punished. After all, his family had huge contacts and they were rich people as well.

After days of rigorous search, the police came to a random decision that Naila and Taruj had fallen victims to a road rage that evening. It was clear to all by then, that Naila and Taruj were actually attacked by strangers in the outskirts of Delhi that evening with a motto of probably looting them, and raping and murdering the girl. Different charges were registered against seven unknown men, as Naila still maintained that she knew none of those men. She also confirmed that she had never seen any of those men near or with Taruj even in his college days. She declined and confirmed that he had no enmity with any of his colleagues as well. With passing days, even the families started believing that strangers had attacked Naila and Taruj that evening when they had planned to get married.

None of them had any more reason not to believe the same, except Naila. She was still not convinced that it all was a result of some road rage. His family was leaving no stones unturned to get the culprits identified and punished. But it was a blind case and that too, a two year old blind case with no leads at all. A month passed by and soon everyone started losing their hopes of ever finding those seven men who were responsible of causing intentional damage to Taruj and Naila. All that they now hoped was to revive Taruj to life once again. While everyone else had given up the hope of finding the culprits, Naila kept alive her hope and was confident that she would soon be in Taruj's arms, and also that the culprits would soon be identified.

His family was not much happy with her presence around him, but none of them rebelled as he started showing speedy recovery in her presence. Time started flying by amidst all the hustle and bustle, and Naila and the family started waiting for the day when they could finally take him home. Tara had moved to Dehradun and Naila had started living with Taruj's eldest sister Astha and her husband and one little son since then. Days started passing by and Naila started spending her life in the hope of once again resting in his strong arms- the arms which were once a house that ended all her worries. While for the others, it was an end, for her it was a new beginning after a painful end. She knew life had something more for her and Taruj even now. She waited and prayed for one fine morning when he would awaken from his deep sleep and take her in his strong arms again, to end all her pains forever, one fine morning when he would stand in front of her in his trademark style- hands behind his neck, smile on his face and crossed legs.

To Be Continued..........

PREETI BHATT

EPILOGOUE

Love has no ending once it begins. The fire of love is warm enough to keep alive the lamps of hope. The hope of meeting what's gone, the hope of reviving what's lost and the hope of healing what's hurt. Love has endless chapters and different seasons to complement each chapter. We fall in love and out of it almost each day. But once we meet our soulmate, life starts making an endless sense. It hardly matters how many times we fall in love and then fall out of it. Only a few chosen ones get the privilege to make love like Naila and Taruj, to make love last forever

ABOUT THE AUTHOR

Preeti Bhatt is a freelance writer who specializes in writing romance. She has done her post graduation in broadcast journalism from Jamia Milia Islamia, New Delhi. She is a gold medalist in broadcast journalism and this is her first book to be published. She has successfully written 7 other novels that await publishing.